Other Copenhagens
(And Other Stories)

By Edmund Jorgensen

Speculation

Other Copenhagens (And Other Stories)

Other Copenhagens (And Other Stories)

by Edmund Jorgensen

Inkwell & Often

Inkwell & Often

ISBN: 0984749209
ISBN-13: 978-0984749201

For Patrick, who makes alternate universes unthinkable

Contents

The Art of Losing

There is no shame in bad hair in and of itself. Bad hair is a hand you're dealt, therefore a hand you can play, sometimes very well. Take Bill Murray, whose hair is like shooting the moon in hearts. Tragic hair, on the other hand, is a choice. Tragic hair is a neglected child or unwatered plant, a crime against beauty, against life itself. The woman in the security footage had tragic hair.

In back it distinguished itself from a football helmet only with an unconvincing wave and halo of split ends. In front the bangs were too long and too evenly cut, and they curled over her forehead like a spookhouse hand reaching across her scalp to poke her in the eye.

Detective Crane rewound the tape and froze it just at the moment when the woman looked up into the camera–or right through the camera, it seemed, through the TV on which the tape was playing, and into the dingy room where I was being questioned.

"Like looking in a mirror, isn't it?" said Detective Crane.

"Only in my nightmares," I said. "Did you see those bangs?"

"So you got your hair cut afterwards."

3

"If I *ever* had those bangs, I'd have to get my *wrists* cut afterwards."

"You're pretty glib for someone caught on video stealing a painting worth ... how much was it?"

"Insured for 200 thousand and change," said Detective Greary.

"200 thousand dollars," said Detective Crane, picking up with perfect rhythm, "and change."

I enjoyed seeing the two of them work together, finishing each other's sentences, setting each other up for lines of questioning. They were well matched physically too: Detective Greary, the eager junior partner who moved and spoke like a minor country music star–without the accent–leaning in the corner, while Detective Crane, pale, jaded and world-worn as one of Goya's soldiers, paced back and forth in front of the table where I was sitting, occasionally leaning in on his knuckles to confront me.

"That's the real crime," I said. "The *Romulus and Remus* is a lousy painting, and anyone who would pay 200K for it has lousy taste. I would have taken the Kandinsky."

"I would be pretty worried in your situation," said Detective Greary, putting his right sole up against the concrete wall and nestling in, "but I have to hand it to you: you don't seem worried."

"Because that's not me."

"You have a twin?" Detective Crane said.

"Is she single?" asked Detective Greary, earning his partner's glare.

"No woman would think for a minute that was me."

4

"Then you should be all set," Detective Crane said. "I'm sure there will be at least one woman on the jury."

"Or you could help us out," said Detective Greary. "This could all go down nice and easy. Tell us where the painting is, and maybe Mr. Firenze will drop the charges. He likes you. He stuck up for you, even after he saw the video. Even after he found out about your history ..."

"My 'history?'"

"It's an illness. People these days get that. Mr. Firenze gets it–I certainly get it."

"You're saying Firenze won't press charges because I'm mentally ill?"

"Hey now," said Detective Greary, tucking in his chin and showing me his palms, as if to demonstrate he held no weapons and came in peace, "you're the one who used those words, not me."

"I was sixteen years old. I went through all the treatment I was ordered, and no one has accused me of stealing anything since."

"Until now," said Detective Crane–a point he thought worth a lean-in.

"We can help you," Detective Greary said, "but you have to help us first."

"If I had wanted that painting, why would I break in the window–why wouldn't I have just stayed late one night and taken it with me?"

"Misdirection," said Detective Crane. "To make us think it was a burglar, not someone who worked at the gallery."

"Then why wouldn't I have turned off the security camera?"

"Maybe you're prettier than you are smart."

5

"I have a smart lawyer, and I want to talk to her."

"Hey now," said Detective Greary again–apparently that was his go-to phrase to slow things down–"things are getting out of hand. We're just chatting here, no reason to get all official. I mean, you call in a lawyer, we have to book you, everything becomes much less fun. Right now this is just a friendly chat, how about we keep it that way?"

"Lawyer."

"Maybe you just tell us some places the painting *might* be–you know, 'If I were a painting, where would I be?' Like a game."

"Lawyer."

"Book her and give her a call," Detective Crane said. He walked out of the interview room without looking back.

"With pleasure," said Detective Greary, after the door had closed.

He chatted me up throughout the entire booking procedure, reminding me periodically in a pro forma tone how much trouble I could still save myself, then following up with a question about which clubs I frequented or what bands I liked. He told me I would look good in orange, twice.

He would have been right on the line for a slow Thursday night at Acuarela. I could imagine him approaching, still in his work clothes, showing off the good strong jaw, the clear blue eyes untroubled by too much intelligence, the sandy hair, and his most attractive attribute: the absurd sureness that I'd let him buy me a drink. I probably would have. With a drink in his hand, he would at least be unable to indulge in his worst habit–the hooking of both thumbs into his belt loops as he spoke. There was some potential there, even if it was buried deep.

"And now," he said, when I had finished my mug shots and fingerprinting, "as promised, your phone call." He handed me a quarter, retracting it at the last moment to add "Don't spend it all in one place."

"Watch me."

I launched the quarter into the pay phone with a flick of the index finger, making sure that it struck the back of the phone hard and fell loudly enough for Detective Greary to hear.

My aunt was unavailable, as always–her assistant said she was in court–so I left a message with a description of my circumstances. Throughout the brief conversation I held the receiver away from my ear, far enough so that Detective Greary would be sure that I was not just talking to a dial tone. I hung up.

"Here's your change," I said, dropping the quarter back into Detective Greary's hand. He looked at the quarter, the phone, then at me, and I smiled innocently as he escorted me to the women's holding area, a man walking his date to her door after an evening gone wrong in some way he could not understand.

The first time it happened I was thirteen years old–or a "baker's dozen years," as my mother had explained to me at my birthday party a few weeks before. It was Easter, and I was sitting in the living room, on the orange sofa that my mother hated but would never replace, kicking my patent leather heels against its flaps and plotting violence against the sleeves of the Easter dress my mother had bought me, which puffed at the shoulders like blowfish trying to swallow my arms and made me look like a pastel linebacker. I was alone–my mother was in the kitchen struggling to get the lamb into the oven, and my father was upstairs shaving, having left the television tuned to the parade, the volume very low, like the murmur of adult conversation from another room.

While I waited for my parents to return, I eyed the chocolates in my basket–forbidden until after dinner–and instead ate a deviled egg from the plate my mother had left on the coffee table, considering all the while whether it would be possible to rend my dress into a sleeveless using only my bare hands, and whether the result would be worth my father's wrath.

My mother returned a few minutes later, wiping sweat from her forehead and tidying her hair. She scanned the living room like a radar dish, hands on her hips, hunting for anything out of place or order, any imperfection which my father might remark on or raise his eyebrows at when he came back down.

"Why can't I have *one* chocolate?" I asked her.

"Have a deviled egg instead. They're your favorite." She angled a picture frame a few inches inward on the mantle.

"I already ate one," I said. "So *now* can I have a chocolate?"

"Bella," she said, moving the frame back to where it had been, "if you don't want an egg, you don't have to eat an egg, but don't lie about it. I can count." She described a small circle with her finger above the plate holding the eggs.

It was an old plate, made of a fine white porcelain that had chipped but not yellowed through the years. Even then I thought the design over-elaborate. The center of the plate bulged into a purely decorative mound of fern-like porcelain leaves, and around the outer edge of the plate porcelain twigs wove in and out of each other like the reeds of a basket. Between these two elements, spaced out evenly around the plate like hours on the face of a clock, twelve egg-shaped depressions in the porcelain waited to cradle a halved egg, fat end towards the center. And, at the moment, all twelve depressions were occupied.

"You made a baker's dozen," I said.

"A baker's dozen is thirteen, remember? Like your age. I made twelve. Let's show off your math–how many eggs did I use if I made twelve?"

"Six."

"Don't roll your eyes, it's good for you to practice. And if I made thirteen?"

"Six and a half."

"That wouldn't make much sense, would it? Where would the other half be?" she said, attempting to tousle my hair. I ducked so she would not feel the dusting of her hairspray I had applied earlier in the bathroom. "All right, have a chocolate, but quick, and don't tell your father."

As I unwrapped a Cadbury Egg I let the matter of the deviled eggs drop, but I knew my mother was mistaken–there must have been thirteen. I could still feel the pickle juice tingling on my lips, and taste paprika. The grainy yolk still coated my tongue.

When my mother died, I inherited the plate. I keep it in the warehouse.

My aunt entered the consultation room like a hurricane, slamming the door, slamming the folder on the table, dumping her coat next to it, and yanking out the chair so it screeched against the floor. She almost parachuted into her seat.

"We had a deal," she said.

"Nice to see you too, Aunt Daniela. I like that cameo–very retro. But I would rethink the pleats on the skirt. You could go straight, or even sheathe–you've still got the legs for it."

"You were supposed to come to me if you started getting those feelings again. You didn't. So explain why I should even agree to represent you, when you broke our deal."

"You aren't even going to ask me if I did it?"

My aunt leaned forward, her elbows on the table, staring at me. I returned her stare until she shook her head and leaned back.

"All right. Did you do it?"

"No."

"Damn it, Bella, I watched the tape."

"You watched the tape, and you still think that was me? Did you *see* those bangs? Does *anyone* in the entire justice system know *anything* about hair?"

She was on her feet again in a second, and the chair slammed back into place below the table.

"I don't have time for games. I have innocent people to defend."

"Maybe I have an alibi," I said. "You didn't even ask."

She was already putting on her coat.

"Do you have an alibi?"

"It was 3 a.m. I was sleeping."

"Alone?"

"That's none of your business."

"Not my business means not an alibi. I was planning to bail you out, but I think maybe a night or two in here will be good for you. I'll see you at the arraignment–you're pleading guilty."

"If you can find a single picture of me with hair like that, ever, I'll gladly plead guilty. As long as I get to serve out my sentence somewhere without mirrors."

"Guard!" my aunt shouted. "We're all done here."

I could not entirely blame my aunt for assuming I was guilty, even in the face of what should have been the sure contraindication of that tragic hair. There was the matter of–as Detective Greary had put it so delicately–my "history."

Back in my high school Cynthia Ward was, inexplicably, the main arbiter of taste for a popular clique of rich girls, and my great enemy on account of the upperclassmen and college freshmen for whose romantic attention we often competed. She did have good taste in men, if not fashion. I used to call her–always to her face–"Skinthia," "Cynthia Weird," and on occasion "Ward of the State," which offended her rich-girl sensibilities deeply and represented my nuclear option. She used to call me "slut" behind my back.

But one day she was not standing far enough behind my back, and the ensuing (rather silly) cat-fight left an image of the thick golden signet-style ring I had carelessly worn that morning imprinted in her mind as

11

well as on her forehead. As luck would have it, she had recently lost her own ring, and during our subsequent dressing down in the principal's office she urged him to put some questions to me that I found it hard to answer, especially when he examined the inside of *my* ring and found engraved there: "Cyn reach for the moon love M & D."

The principal's report to my mother prompted a toss of my room, where she discovered the underwear drawer in which I kept all the jewelry–my first warehouse–and, since I could not explain how I had come by these pieces, it was decided that I must have stolen them. My father, always one for Truth and Justice Equally for All Amen and God Bless America, reported me to the police over my mother's lamentations, and turned all the jewelry over to them. As I was a minor, and the police had trouble determining the identity of my supposed victims, I never saw the inside of anything more serious than a therapist's office. But even in that office I did face an unpleasant choice.

I like the truth. I prefer it to lies, all things being equal, as I prefer simpler cuts in dresses and fewer accessories in outfits. These are guidelines to depart from only with good reason. But in truth, as in fashion, there are both eternal and seasonal principles at play. There are no hard and fast rules to memorize and be done with–"always tell the truth"–"never wear dangly earrings with shoulder straps." The situation is always fluid, and the human factor cannot be overestimated: with a few changed minds high fashion can become kitsch, or the truth a lie. So I could choose either to tell my therapist a truth he could never have believed, and therefore be a liar; or to lie to him, and be just a young woman with an intense attraction to beautiful things and an underdeveloped notion of personal property. Not much of a choice, really.

To this day I attend the odd meeting at my local chapter of Kleptomaniacs Anonymous. I still have some friends there, and recovering kleptomaniac men, who live straddling the border of adrenaline and repressed desire, know how to show a girl a good evening or two.

At my arraignment Monday morning I pleaded not guilty, and made arrangements for my bail.

Aunt Daniela was so angry she wouldn't speak to me on the way out of the court room. I followed her through the halls and out the doors of the building, trying to talk to her, until we were halfway down the court house steps.

"Fine," I shouted. "Go on. If I need to talk to you I'll just get arrested again–that seems to be the only way you have the time of day for me."

She stopped short at the bottom corner of the stairs, right by the statue of Justice, and turned around to look at me. I always forgot how beautiful my aunt really was–she had the same features as my mother, but she wore them differently, as if the same material had gone into a smart pants suit instead of a summer frock. At that moment, however, in the thin light of a New York spring morning, she seemed just as beautiful and permanent as the statue of Justice holding up her scales–and just as undecided. She started to say something, bit her lip, and then continued.

"I'll stop by tonight. Be home."

She turned and walked away, shaking her head.

I waited until she was out of sight before I hailed the cab.

"Red Hook," I said, and, just to be on the safe side, gave an address a few blocks away from my destination.

My caution paid off: I was in front of Jerry's Tavern, just a block from the warehouse, when I spotted him over my shoulder.

"Hello, Detective Greary," I called.

He came sheepishly out of the alley into which he had retreated too late and crossed over to my side of the street, waving a passing taxi in front of him.

"Buy you a drink?" I said, motioning my head back at the sign for Jerry's.

"It's 11:30 in the morning."

"It's 11:45. And that's not an answer."

"I'm on duty."

"That's not an answer either."

He shrugged and opened the door, holding it for me.

Jerry's Tavern had no windows, and only the bare minimum of bulbs, so it took a few seconds for our vision to adjust. When it did, Detective Greary whistled.

"These are the real professionals," he said. There were only three other customers in the bar, all of them men, all of them gray and beige and lumpy, too intent on their own drinks and misery to even notice our entrance.

"These are sad people who drink alone," I said. "Be nice, or you'll be drinking alone too."

He grumbled at the chastening, but went to order two beers from the bar while I staked a claim to one of the high tables in the corner.

"So, Detective Greary," I said as he set the drinks down, "what brings you out to Red Hook? There's not much to see out here, unless you like dingy taverns and warehouses."

"Mark."

"Get set, go?"

"Call me Mark."

"You're on duty–right, Detective Greary? Are you on the job too?"

"Just call me Mark. What do you mean, on the job?"

"I mean we didn't just end up on the same street in Red Hook at 11:45 on a Monday morning by accident. Were you hoping I would lead you to the painting?"

"Why else would I be following you?"

I took a sip of my beer, which sparkled with unusually large bubbles, as if it had been diluted with seltzer. It tasted about like seltzer too.

"There are two ways to interpret this scene," I said. "Maybe you're a detective following a suspect, hoping she'll lead you to some stolen property. In which case we'll finish this beer and then I'll head home and wait for a time when you're not following me to do what I need to do. Or maybe you're just a man on an errand who ran into a woman on another errand. In which case, we could have another drink tonight. Or dinner."

He took the first sip of his own beer and made a face. Something in the taste seemed to make him aware of the flat, stale smell of the place, and he wrinkled his nose.

"It's not that easy," he said.

"It's not that hard, either. Would this make it easier? I didn't take that painting."

"Then what are you doing out here?"

"Trust isn't your strong point, is it?"

"A trusting nature isn't usually what drives someone to become a cop."

"But you like me."

He refused to meet my eyes.

"And you're not totally convinced I did it, are you?" I said. "Even with the video. Why?"

He shrugged.

"You see a lot of liars in this line of work. Most people are terrible liars, but every once in a while you run across someone who knows how to tell a lie so that it doesn't sound like a lie–and that's enough to fool most people, because that's what most people are listening for–'does this sound like a lie?' But as a cop, you learn to listen for the *truth*, which is a whole different ball game. A good lie doesn't sound like a lie, yeah–but only the truth sounds like the truth."

"I see, so it's all about authenticity."

"That's right."

"The real thing."

"There ain't nothing like it," he said, and clinked his bottle against mine where it stood on the table–a silly gesture, but I liked the confidence it showed.

"What if there were?" I asked him.

"Sorry?"

"For example, what's your favorite painting?"

"I don't really think I have a favorite–painting isn't really my thing."

"So you mean your favorite is Van Gogh's *Starry Night*."

He paused, a swallow of beer still in his mouth, and looked at me, baffled.

"No, I don't read minds," I said. "It's just that every tough guy I've ever met secretly loved *Starry Night*. It was probably on the wall of their dorm room, and it's the image on their computer desktop until their favorite Rottweiler dies and bumps it. But none of them will admit that they like the painting, because they seem to think it would be tantamount to getting caught reading a romance novel in the locker room. So, painting's not your thing, got it, but if, hypothetically, you could buy *Starry Night*, would you do it?"

"Legally?"

"Could you pretend for 30 seconds that you're not a cop? Yes, legally."

"I don't know what you think cops make, but I don't see that happening."

"For God's sake, show some imagination. Pretend you had billions and billions of dollars–money you earned through some totally legal enterprise–would you buy *Starry Night* for 50 million? That's a very good price, by the way–probably less than half of what it's worth."

"Sure, I guess I would buy it and hang it in my yacht. Is that the answer you want?"

This was not the time to lecture him on what salt-water air could do to oil and canvas.

"Fine, so you'd buy it. Now let's say you could buy a *copy* of *Starry Night*–a perfect copy–I mean down to the last detail, absolutely indistinguishable from the original, by even the biggest experts in the field with electron microscopes and what-have-you–for the same price. Would you do it?"

"Of course not."

"Even though it's exactly the same–meaning it's just as good a painting. Think about it."

"No," he said, without thinking about it.

"Why not?"

"Because it's fake. A forgery."

"Wrong," I said. "You wouldn't buy it because you are an essentialist."

"I've been called a lot of things in my day, but never an . . . ?"

"Essentialist. It means you believe physical things have an essential character. They pick up histories. Don't worry, you're not alone. Basically the whole human species is essentialist. It's why you wouldn't wear Hitler's sweater, even if it were a very nice sweater and laundered 100 times and dry cleaned and sterilized and rinsed with holy water–which is totally an essentialist concept, by the way–which had been blessed by the Pope himself."

"I'm not much of a sweater guy."

"Fine, Hitler's cowboy boots, then."

"Cowboy boots? Really? What did I ever do to you?"

"Besides book me for grand theft? But fine, you wouldn't wear Hitler's manly, awesome leather holster. Or spend his gold! My point is, don't you think that's strange, when all these things are–according to science–just an arrangement of atoms? It's not like we're fetishists for atoms–one carbon atom is as good as another–so you'd think it would be the *arrangement* that mattered to us. But no. If some other atoms are arranged in exactly the same way, we say 'no, that's not *Starry Night*, that's something different, a forgery.' As if the atoms were important, not the arrangement. But that can't be right. Look at us ... we're replacing our own atoms all the time. Are you a different person than you were yesterday, just because some of your atoms are different? Of course not. You're an arrangement. That's what matters with people. So why not with a painting?"

Detective Greary made a show of taking a stiff drink. "You have a way of making a man's head spin," he said.

"I'm just getting warmed up, Detective Greary."

"Mark."

We fell into an awkward silence, and I let him stew as he pretended to sip at his beer, his gaze alternating between me and the back of the bar.

"Mark," I said, "you've been eyeing the bathroom since we came in here. Just go."

"And have you give me the slip?"

"I'll still be here when you get out. Scout's honor."

"That's the Vulcan sign for 'live long and prosper.' It doesn't exactly inspire confidence."

"What if I give you my word?"

"Please," he said. I liked the confident tilt of his head as he said it. He was so much more attractive when he was suspicious.

"Then how about ... "

I reached down to my left below the high table.

"... if I give you ... "

I reached down on the other side.

"… a collateral?"

I dangled both of my shoes from my right hand, the heels hooked on my index and middle fingers.

"Come on, Detective Greary, no one is going to walk around Red Hook in stockings. The hypodermics alone!"

"I'm not sure I really want to be seen carrying high heels into a men's room in a place like this."

"You struck me as a man who was more secure in his masculinity than that–*Starry Night* aside."

"It's not my masculinity that I'm worried about."

But he took the shoes from me one by one, letting his fingers brush against mine as he did so. As he walked over to the men's room, he paused twice to look back. The third time, I waved and smiled.

As soon as the door had closed behind him, I took a pen from my purse, scribbled a note on his napkin, and left, my high heels rapping against the dusty wooden floor of Jerry's Tavern so loudly that even the day-drinkers looked up.

After concluding my business in Red Hook, and a brief stop at Hoeffner's Fine Art Repairs and Restorations in Chelsea, I waited as the afternoon warmed up on the last bench on Central Park West, watching the building across the street until Virginia Firenze came out of it. She was carrying her gym bag and yoga mat, as she did every Monday afternoon, and from the stoop she gave the usual nervous scan of the sidewalk that I had long since realized was not fear of being assaulted or approached for a drug buy, but of running into someone she knew in the art world who might look at her in her unitard, then at the building she had just come out of, and suddenly understand why she and Gustavo Firenze always entertained in the gallery, never in their home, and always reported their home as "Central Park West" without a number or cross street. As soon as she had rounded the corner and disappeared into the subway entrance, I crossed the street and rang the first floor apartment.

"Bella!" said Gustavo Firenze, opening the door to meet me in the hall after he had buzzed me in. As angry as I was with him, I still enjoyed hearing my name rendered in his light Italian accent. "Come in, come in! I am so glad that you have come." He ushered me in, peering around me for his wife.

"You don't look glad."

He always looked shorter at home than at work, as if his merely being in the gallery gave him two-inch platforms. But his apartment, even if it was on the first floor and clinging on to Central Park West for dear life, was impeccably decorated–a Parisian salon made modern with prominent blacks and whites. He was wearing a deep green velvet jacket, which picked up the landscape tints from the Bril on the wall behind him and put him in a dead heat for "most colorful object in the room."

"Of course I am glad you have come, but I am not happy, how could I be? Such a disaster, a nightmare this whole business has been. I have not slept in days, not a wink. You must know how terrible I feel."

"So terrible that you pressed charges?"

"Sit, sit, you will fray my nerves otherwise. Virginia insisted that we press charges, over my most strenuous objections. What was I to say? Please, tell me. You have seen the video. The woman is like your twin but with terrible hair. I told the police those were not your bangs but they would not listen. What terrible, no, what infernal bad luck! How could I explain to Virginia that she was not you?"

"You mean, how could you explain it to her without mentioning that, at the exact moment that video was taken, you had me bent over a bed on the third floor of the Mercer?"

"So vulgar when you are angry. Is that how you think of the beautiful connection between us?"

"How should I think of it, Gustavo? You let me spend two nights in jail and then go through an arraignment, all for something you know I couldn't have done."

"I promise you that I slept worse than you could have those two nights, my treasure. I am in a different kind of jail—one from which there is no simple release. My heart is one jail, my marriage another."

"If this goes to trial, I'll have no choice but to tell where I really was that night."

"How can you say such things? You know of Virginia's heart condition—that would kill her."

"What condition, that she was born without a heart? You mean that *she* would kill *you*. Or worse: divorce you and take the gallery."

"We will find a resolution to this, Bella. We will find a way as we always have, together. Perhaps I can slip you some money—as much as the painting is worth—and then we can settle out of court, for that amount. It will cost you nothing, no one will ever have to know."

"I know you don't have 200 thousand lying around, Gustavo. I do the books for the gallery, remember? I'm the one who tells you no one came in all day. You hardly made rent last month."

"There are always other sources of money–one must be creative, it is the key to life."

"I'm not going to admit to something I didn't do."

"No, there will be no admission of wrongdoing. Only we will settle out of court, and there will be an end to it."

"And I keep my job?"

Firenze grew agitated, standing and beginning to pace.

"I will pour you a drink," he said.

"In other words, no. But you'll still happily fuck me during Yoga Mondays and every other Thursday night while your wife visits with her mother in White Plains, right?"

He covered his ears and moaned, as if I had poured acid into them.

"Oh! How can you use such words with me? You must know that I could not keep you on at the gallery–Virginia would never allow it. But I would find something else for you–a new job, a better job somewhere."

"Tell me all about this other gallery that will hire me after you fire me for being an art thief."

"But if we settle out of court, no one will ever need to know. I will make sure that Virginia never breathes a word. And most importantly, even if we cannot work together any longer–which breaks my heart–our deeper, more significant connection can continue, yes?"

"You're unbelievable," I said. "Let me propose a different plan. First of all, it's over between us. Second of all, you're going to remember that a prospect spilled tea on the *Romulus and Remus* Wednesday, which you forgot about until the early hours of Thursday. You then called me at 3 a.m., waking me from a sound sleep, and demanded on pain of termination that I return to the gallery *right then* to retrieve the painting so I could bring it in first thing for an emergency cleaning at Hoeffner's.

"I was so shaken up that I got all the way to the gallery before I realized that, of course, I don't have a key. I called you and you insisted that I break the window and take the painting. So all of this is an unfortunate misunderstanding, and entirely your fault for forgetting about those late night phone calls–during which, by the way, you were drunk and verbally abusive.

"Finally, despite your *extremely* public lamentations and apologies, I'm going to start looking for a new job, and until I find it you're going to continue to pay me my current salary. And in return for these considerations, I'll make sure that no one–especially Virginia–ever finds out where you were at 3 a.m. last Thursday, or two Thursdays before that, or before that, and so on. You get the picture?"

He adjusted his collar, and the cast of his face hardened.

"A charming plan, to be sure, charming, if a bit fanciful. But haven't you forgotten one small detail, my treasure? You don't have the painting. It might be very difficult to sell your story without the painting. If you were to say unkind things about me publicly, I might be forced to do the same–for the sake of my marriage, you see, though it would break my heart–and then you would just have the word of a suspected art thief with–pardon me for mentioning–your troubled history, against the word of a respected New York gallery owner."

"Here," I said, standing up.

"What is this?"

"Your claim at Hoeffner's–the Chelsea office. Don't worry, the dates will check out just fine, I've taken care of it."

"This is impossible–you cannot have the painting–you were with me."

"But it's happening."

"I don't understand."

"Poor Gustavo," I said. I stood on my tiptoes and kissed the top of his head, right in the bald spot. "There's so much you don't understand, and never will."

Aunt Daniela arrived at my apartment just after six, blowing through the door like a warm front, a bag of groceries in each arm. She kissed me on the cheek as she passed.

"How do you live in this clutter, Bella? Where's your stereo? I need opera when I cook."

"I'm not sure I have any opera."

She set down the bags on the counter of my walk-in kitchen and produced a CD of Verdi from her purse.

"I never travel into cultural backwaters without it. Put this on for me. And then stay out–the kitchen is mine."

"There's something we need to talk about."

"Oh," said Aunt Daniela, looking over her shoulder, "don't worry. I know all about the developments today, and we're going to have a long conversation about a good many things over dinner. Where is your saucepan?"

"Which one is a saucepan again?"

"Where are your knives?"

"The knife is in the left drawer."

"*The* knife? You're hopeless. Just put on the opera and let me do my thing." She began to pull plum tomatoes from one of the bags and pile them next to the sink.

"What am I supposed to do in the meantime?"

"What would you do if I weren't here?"

"Order dinner."

"Then find something else to do. Out!"

Sitting in the living room I picked through a Cosmo as the smell of sauteed onion and stewing tomatoes filled the apartment. After a while I closed my eyes and, with the unmistakable sense that I would pay for this luxury, allowed myself to imagine that I was twelve again, back home, wasting time in the living room while my mother cooked her ragù. The Verdi on high volume was different–my father would never have stood for it–but behind the quivering sopranos and impassioned tenors, my aunt's tuneless humming could have been my mother's. After a few minutes of this I had to flee to the bathroom to get a hold of myself.

"This is more carbs than I've had in a year," I said, sopping up the ragù from my third helping of gemelli with fresh Italian bread.

"Glad you liked it," said Aunt Daniela. She was still picking at her own first serving, but had paced me with the red wine, never questioning the appearance of the second bottle.

About halfway through that second bottle she began to tell some of the stories about my mother as a girl: the time she hid her father's wallet to punish him for hitting the dog; how she ran away and slept in the church the night of her first kiss; how she drank holy water after she lied to her mother about stealing her lipstick. Then her own drunken confessions began.

"For a long time I thought your mother was the weak one. I looked down on her. I'm just being honest! I was going to study law and save innocent people from suffering at the hands of a corrupt system. I was going to right wrongs and further the cause of justice. Meanwhile your mother was going to get married and win the blue ribbon in the meringue category at the church bake sale. But life never works out like you expect, Bella. Now I think of my clients as guilty until proven innocent. Sometimes even after they're proven innocent. I can't even pinpoint when that changed, when I got so jaded.

"And that's not even the worst part–the worst part is the self pity–the feeling that somehow I've been cheated or tricked, when of course I've made my own decisions all along, and refused to listen to anyone. I guess it turned out I didn't have much of a stomach for reality. But your mother? I never heard her complain, not once. Not with all that crap your father put her through, or when Mr. Moral himself ran off with his slut. Not when she got sick. Not even when she found out–when she found out she wouldn't get better. She always did what she could with what she had at hand."

Aunt Daniela poured the dregs of the second bottle into her glass.

"Speaking of which, young lady, do you want to explain to me how that painting miraculously resurfaced?"

"Not particularly."

"Uh huh. And is there anything you want to tell me about Firenze?"

"Firenze?"

"Maybe about him and the Mercer hotel, and where you were during the time the surveillance video was taken?"

"That little weasel."

"He folded like a chair," she said with unsteady professional pride. "Squealed like a ... like a ... " Her eyes unfocused for a moment as she suddenly and visibly descended a rung on the ladder of intoxication.

"Pig?" I offered.

"Canary," she said with triumph. "But there's still something fishy about the whole business. Firenze calling you out of nowhere, telling you to break the glass, 'forgetting' that the painting was being cleaned. I think he was trying to set you up, that's what I think."

She tried to pour more from the empty bottle until I gently confiscated it from her.

"I'm pretty sure that's not what's going on, Aunt Daniela, though I appreciate the maternal attitude."

"The point is," she said, steadying herself and her glass, "that I wish I had believed you sooner. But anyone who saw that video would have thought you were stealing that painting."

"Even someone who didn't know I was a recovering kleptomaniac."

"Recovered."

"We're not allowed to say recovered."

"But why didn't you just tell me the truth? Why that whole dog and pony show about your hair and everything?"

"Would you have believed me? Honestly?"

My aunt swirled the last drops of wine around her glass.

"Probably not," she said. "I'm sorry to say it, but that's the truth. Probably not. But hey," she continued, brightening, "you should have seen Detective Crane when he found out. He was fit to be tied–that guy *really* wants to charge someone. He even asked me if you had an undocumented twin."

"Did you tell him?"

"Did I tell him what?"

"That you and my mother were twins."

My aunt sat up, stock straight, as though she had just tossed back a hangover remedy heavy on the horseradish and jumped into a cold shower at the same time. Her eyes widened and then narrowed. I knew what was happening–I had seen it before. The unwritten rule had been broken–only she was allowed to mention my mother. The hurt was still too raw when someone else brought her up.

"Why on earth would I tell him that?"

29

"I don't know–I thought he might find it an amusing coincidence."

"It's late," said my aunt. "I have to go." She stood, balancing herself on the table until she remembered how to use her legs.

"Fine."

I helped her gather her things and walked her to the door, where she surprised me, breaking the discomfort with a fierce hug.

"I'll try to stop by more often," she said into my ear. "By the way, I'm glad you cut your hair–it looks much better like this."

As she released me I opened the door for her, but she had noticed something over my shoulder, and was staring at it with a look on her face that I could not easily classify. Her expression would not have seemed out of place either in a wedding album or among the pews at a funeral. I turned to see what had captivated her: the mirror on the antique hall tree. Right away I saw what she saw there–saw how the reflection of my aunt in that old mirror, with its threads of missing silver around the edges, was no longer my aunt, but my mother. It was unbearable to look at, so I turned instead to where my own reflection should have been–but I could no longer say who it was that I saw looking back at me.

It was almost 11:30 when I arrived at Acuarela. The crowd was light, but not too unusual for a Monday, and more people were on the floor than at the bars or tables. DJ Romantik was spinning his weird medleys of Depression-era jazz and techno, which, as always, seemed remarkably less profound to me when I was without chemical assistance.

I slid into a spot at the central bar (I had never seen the point of the more private corner bars, where no one could see you) and proceeded to wait–wait!–for almost five minutes.

"Rudolfo, what the hell is this?" I asked as he tried to sneak past me. "I have to wait for a drink now?"

"All right, Bella, one more, but just one–and take this one slow, yeah?" He began agitating the shaker.

Before I could answer him, an arm reached around me and slapped a cocktail napkin on the zinc bar. It soaked up the ring of water sweated off an earlier patron's drink, so the ink started to bleed, but my handwriting was still legible: "Acuarela, 10:00."

"Well?" said Detective Greary, swinging into position beside me, his back against the bar. As he spoke he refused to look at me, staring instead out at the thin sea of bodies moving to DJ Romantik's whims.

"Well what?"

"Which apology would you like to make first? I'm flexible."

"Man," I said, picking up the drink Rudolfo slid across to me, "are you in for a long night."

"First of all, there's the fact that you wasted an hour of my time–and my partner's–sitting in Interview Room Four and playing games with us, swearing up and down that wasn't you in the video–when, as we now know, it was–and conveniently failing to mention as well that you were there on Firenze's instructions. Supposedly, that is–I have some lingering questions about that scenario."

"It's good to preserve some mystery–that's what makes life worth living."

"So second we have your ditching me this morning. Some people might consider that your worst offense, but I have a professional appreciation for that one. I mean, the patience of waiting for me to hit the bathroom–the whole bit with the shoes. That was well played. And then leaving this note with a place and time, which is almost like an apology–or an IOU for an apology. How am I doing so far?"

"There are no words to describe your understanding of the female mind."

"Then third we have the whole 'tell him to be there at 10 and I'll waltz in at 10:30' thing, which is an interesting one. On the one hand, you could argue that showing up late to a date you made when you ditched someone is worse than ditching them in the first place. But on the other hand, men have always waited around for women and always will. She's trying on her tenth outfit and he's already in the car. Who am I to go against tradition? So I say that's not really apology number one. With me so far?"

"Except that it's 11:30, not 10:30."

"But the one I really don't get–the one that makes me question what I'm even doing here talking to you–even in that dress–is pretending not to know me."

"This is what you call pretending not to know you? What were you expecting, exactly? Sex in the bathroom?"

"I'm not talking about now–I'm talking about when I came in. You were up there"–he pointed to the balcony–"looking down, and you saw me, clear as day, and you saw me wave to you. I thought you were coming down to join me, but instead I have to track you down for an hour. So yeah, now that I say it out loud, I'm pretty sure that's your first apology."

"Save my spot," I said, handing him my drink.

"Where are you going?"

"Seriously? To the bathroom. Do I need a hall pass?"

"No no no," he said, "we don't have a good history with the bathroom. And no, I won't take your shoes as collateral. I've seen this movie before."

"How about my dress?"

"You serious?"

"No."

His face fell.

"If you've got to go," he said, "you go. But then I'm out of here."

"Suit yourself. Shame to cut short what could have been a lovely evening." I stood up on my tiptoes (I did like his height), took the tips of his collar between my index fingers and thumbs, and kissed him briefly on the mouth. Then I walked straight to the ladies' room without looking back, to show him how that was done, just in case he might still prove trainable.

I had not been waiting for her more than a minute or two before she stumbled into the bathroom, visibly over-served. She had fixed her hair–I was glad to see that–but her dress was a disaster, a sherbet lime green A-line that even a moderately self-respecting bridesmaid wouldn't be caught dead in. How could Detective Greary, who was presumably trained in observation, have confused that with my black Versace strapless? That might be strike three for the good detective.

She stood next to me in front of the sinks, one basin over, the two of us looking askance at each other in the mirror. A blonde in business casual came through the door giggling and talking on her cell, but seemed to sense something was not right and turned around. I locked the door and returned to the sinks. We were alone.

I watched her for a minute in the mirror, cringing whenever she swayed or moved in some way I had not, as if my reflection were defecting. I could not explain why it disturbed me so deeply when she blinked, until I realized: I had never seen my eyelids in a mirror before.

"Are you me?" I said finally.

She laughed–not my pleasant laugh, the one I used to secure an invitation, but the one I used to end an evening prematurely. Her eyes scrunched up meanwhile, and I had to look away. Did I look that pinched and unattractive when I laughed? I must.

"I know you're deciding whether to kill me right now," she said. Hearing her was as strange and familiar as hearing my own voice recorded. "But I don't blame you. The first time I saw you my instinct was to smother you under one of your many pillows."

"You were in my bedroom?"

"Wednesday morning I was eating cereal in my apartment. Then I was eating cereal in your apartment. At first I did not understand what had happened. I thought all my lovely objects had come back to me–there was my oak coffee table, and the crystal horse-and-cart salt cellar that I couldn't resist buying upstate, even though I knew you would call it to you. But certain details were off: I did not recognize the clothes strewn over the sofa, or the bronze cupid where you hang your keys. And then I found you in the bedroom, wearing your satin blindfold, with your second duvet kicked to the ground, and I understood. You had finally called me to you, as you had called all my lovely objects. You look confused."

"Those were yours?"

"Where did you think they came from?"

"I didn't think they came *from* anywhere. I thought they were just ... copies. Doubles."

"I've always known you must be out there, calling my things to you. You never even guessed about me–not even once?"

She appeared distraught, as if, after a lifetime of my having taken things from her, this slight was the one injury she could not forgive.

"Maybe I suspected," I said, "once. Or at least wondered. It was the day after my mother died, and I was sitting in Riverside Park, looking out at the water, holding ... "

"My mother's silver cross."

"Yes, my mother's silver cross, the one she was wearing when she died, and then–I was holding two of them, and the second was already warm, as if ... "

"As if someone had been holding it? Gripping it tightly, for dear life? Praying furiously that this one thing, just this one thing, would not be snatched away?"

"And I wondered, just for a moment, whose hand had made it warm. I'm sorry." What else was there to say?

35

She shrugged in the mirror, and I felt my own shoulders tense.

"The art of losing isn't hard to master. I've learned how to live. I sit down lightly, half expecting the chair to vanish. I carry extra pens."

"So why didn't you kill me?"

She squirmed a bit.

"I don't know. Fear at first. Then–perhaps–anger. Maybe I thought that would be too easy–that I wanted to take other things from you than your life, things that might hurt you more."

"You mean you wanted to get me thrown into jail by implicating me in an art theft?"

"That was foolish of me–petty. I knew that even as I was doing it. When I had some time to think, walking around the city these last few days, I realized what I really wanted."

"Which was what?"

"This. To meet you–to make you aware of me. To see you, talk to you. To touch you."

She stretched her hand along the bank of sinks, but I moved mine away.

"Well, now you've met me," I said. "But you still haven't answered my first question–are we the same person? Two copies of the same person? I mean, do you work in a gallery in ... wherever you come from? Were you having an affair with your boss? Do we like the same foods? Did you study art history?"

"As a child I loved art–art and pretty frocks and silver chains, lovely objects of all kinds. But you were always calling them to you, taking my drawings before I had even finished them, or stranding me in a public bathroom without a blouse. Like a weaker

36

sister defining herself I changed my tastes–I learned to love poetry instead of the plastic arts, and now I teach literature. Or I did. You might take a book from me, but once I had committed a poem to memory, then even you could not take it. A poem is all arrangement and no atoms. And I changed my taste in clothes, finding styles I knew you would never call to you–garish colors and vulgar cuts. Only the ugly shoes, those I could never learn to love. So I travel with extra pairs."

"So we're not the same person."

"I did not say that. I have thought long and hard, and I believe there cannot be two of us. If human beings are not paintings, neither are we poems. We have histories. We cannot be just the arrangement and not the atoms. So there is only one original–and I suppose that must be you. After all, if the lovely objects are called to you–if even I am called to you–how can you not be the real us?"

We stood in silence for a few minutes, a look of pain on her face, until I couldn't stand any more.

"Here," I said, sliding the key along the bank of sinks, careful not to let her hand brush mine. "It's in Red Hook–the address is taped on top. You'll find your things there, and some money. But then you have to go–get a moving truck or something and get out of New York."

She examined the key, rubbing it like a talisman, and put it to her lips before pocketing it.

"I'll go for now," she said. "But I can't say how long I will be able to stay away. You may call all my things to you again–or you might call me myself."

"You understand–if you come back, you won't leave me any choice."

"I understand. Perhaps neither of us has any choice."

She leaned in towards me and seemed to grow large and terrible, a blur of lime green that I could not escape. My head began to swim–I reached out to steady myself on the sink. Then she kissed me–her lips against mine like a static shock–and I passed out.

"Bella? Bella?"

Detective Greary was crouched over me on the floor, calling my name and snapping his fingers.

"Hey," he said as I stirred, "welcome back. You had us worried for a second."

As the bathroom came back into focus, I saw a small crowd of women standing in the doorway, hands over their mouths.

"Did you take something, Bella?" Detective Greary asked.

"No."

"You sure about that?"

"Yes."

"All right, not so fast, let me help you up. Let's take our time with this. You feeling all right?"

"I'm fine," I croaked, pushing him away, but I was not.

My voice sounded like a recording. My lips still tingled warmly, as though I had glossed them with something caustic, and the raw skin there could actually feel itself against itself, as if it belonged to someone else.

"Easy," he said. "Easy there. I need to check your pupils, can you open up those beautiful eyes for me?"

He cajoled, teased, even commanded, but I refused, shaking my head, crying and screaming and thrashing until he had to restrain me. I couldn't open my eyes, I wouldn't, not for him or anything or anyone. I could not bear to confirm what I had already seen in the corner of my vision–there where the elegant lines of black Versace should have been, instead of that terrible flash–impossible to unsee–of sherbet lime green.

And Not Your Yellow Hair

Thursday

On a crisp October morning in an industrial park some twenty miles west of Boston, Janine Smalls parked her rental car astride two handicapped spaces, hung up on her agent Maurice in mid-protest, and with the small, angry steps necessitated by the height of her heels and the fit of her skirt, walked up to the squat concrete building and yanked at the door.

Before she could even register the indignity of having found it locked, Miss Smalls saw movement through the smoked glass and a face floated up like a startled fish to the surface of a pond, the nose leaving a smudge on the glass between the white stenciled words "Educated" and "Alternatives."

Having unlocked and opened the door so energetically as to almost knock Miss Smalls over in the process, the receptionist (whose face it was) wove her repeated apologies for the locked door so densely between her offers to take the actress's jacket (accepted) and the silk scarf which covered her head (declined), and to bring her a bottle of the Italian bottled water that the gossip mags reported Miss Smalls would only accept sealed and at "cellar temperature" (accepted), that when she asked Miss Smalls if she would like anything else as she waited, the actress replied "No more apologies would be just fantastic."

The receptionist, holding back tears, picked up the phone to report Miss Smalls's arrival, and fifteen seconds later at the most Jerome Pope, co-founder and CEO of Educated Alternatives, burst through the swinging door that connected the back office with reception.

Before the doors had even stopped swinging he had managed: to welcome Miss Smalls; to thank the receptionist; to chide her for not having taken the silk scarf covering the actress's hair; to acknowledge Miss Smalls's continued refusal to part with the same; and to suggest that she accompany him to the conference room, where they could "chat more comfortably." He caught the door on an inswing and held it open, scooping his arm forward and glaring at the receptionist after Miss Smalls had passed.

Jerome Pope was a tailor's dream: a short, portly gentleman who renovated his wardrobe every year or ten pounds, whichever came first–a contest whose outcome was annually in doubt. He was not ashamed of his belly. To the contrary, he wielded it like a forceful avatar, a herald of his imminent arrival, and Miss Smalls appreciated this lack of shame. It suggested that he "owned his body"–an attitude for which she had professional admiration. As she followed him down the hall, she imagined the call that might cast him.

Fast-talking Harvard graduate gone to seed in his 40s, big personality, bigger appetites, making a last grab at the brass ring.

"This is Dr. Novak, my co-founder and our Chief Science Officer," said Mr. Pope, having offered Miss Smalls a seat in the windowless conference room at the end of the hall. "Miss Smalls, of course, requires no introduction."

Dr. Novak, to the actress's displeasure, had not even made a modest effort to look the part of the mad scientist. He wore neither lab coat or glasses, and his sweater vest and slacks–while detectably wrinkled–were recently laundered, reasonably sized, and passably matched.

"Does he need to be here?" asked Miss Smalls. "My meeting was with you."

"I am merely the face of our little operation," said Mr. Pope, sitting down in the third chair at the small table. "Dr. Novak is the brain–the chef who dreamed up our secret sauce, if you will, and the only man alive who really knows how to stir and season it. Without him, we could not do what we do."

"Which is what, exactly?"

"You came to us at the recommendation of Governor Schwarzenegger–what did he tell you?"

"Something I didn't believe."

"You must have at least wondered, or you wouldn't have driven up from New York to meet us. What did he tell you?"

"He told me," said Miss Smalls, appearing to choose her words carefully, "that you helped him win re-election."

"Did he say how? You may stop regarding Dr. Novak with such suspicion," said Mr. Pope. "We really do need him here."

Something in the way he said this struck Miss Smalls as directorial–as if Mr. Pope were giving a note on her performance–and the actress in her decided to follow where he was leading the scene.

"Governor Schwarzenegger said that you can see the future."

Dr. Novak laughed and shifted in his seat.

"These 'clients' you bring in don't even understand what I do at a basic level," he said to Mr. Pope.

"You must forgive my colleague, Miss Smalls," said Mr. Pope, looking at Dr. Novak rather than Miss Smalls as he spoke. "In your line of work you cannot be unfamiliar with the difficult genius–perhaps you have even been painted with that brush once or twice yourself. Dr. Novak is precise to a fault, and lacks a certain social grace, but he is undoubtedly a genius. And in fact, you're not so far off–what goes on within these walls is not quite seeing the future–but it *is* the stuff of science fiction. Dr. Novak, would you do the honors?"

"Why me, when you always do it so much better?" said the scientist. But Mr. Pope merely sat smiling, and at length Dr. Novak gave up and turned to Miss Smalls.

"Do you know what a parallel universe is?" he asked.

"Of course she does," said Mr. Pope. "She starred in *Thymelines*."

"Timelines?"

"With an 'h' and 'y'–like the herb."

"Ah. I must have missed that one."

"It's about an up-and-coming chef who wakes up one morning and has her life split along two different paths," said Miss Smalls. "In one she succeeds in the culinary world but is never fulfilled personally. In the other her restaurant closes, but she finds love. Then at the end you see her back in her bed, right before her life splits, and you can tell by the look on her face that she's just fully experienced both of these two lives somehow, like a dream, and is getting a second chance to choose between them. It's powerful. It's funny you should mention that movie, it's been on my mind a lot lately."

"Let me guess which life she chooses," said Dr. Novak. "All right, so that's a parallel universe as a tired cinematic plot device. Real life is different–no one wakes up in bed and experiences two timelines. Parallel universes are a real thing, but they're–well, parallel. You're stuck in one universe or the other, and you can't even see the others. But you *can* model them as lines in a common Hilbert space, with the consequence that ... "

"Or at least," said Mr. Pope, "you *couldn't* see them–until our own Dr. Novak arrived on the scene. He is too modest to admit the enormity of his achievement–and perhaps too brilliant to ever condescend to explain it in layman's terms, beg him as I might. But these parallel universes are not only real, they are proximate–they are right here, in this room ... "

Dr. Novak tensed his shoulders.

"... but we cannot touch, taste, smell, hear these universes–even though, I assure you, they are *right here* ... "

Mr. Pope reached out his hand and rubbed his thumb against the pads of his index and middle fingers, as if to verify that he could feel no parallel universe there, and then opened his hand to show that he had palmed no universes meanwhile.

"... because they are separated from us by dimensions that are not the dimensions of our familiar space and time–dimensions that we cannot even travel in, Miss Smalls. Do you understand?"

Miss Smalls would not have described the feeling she had as "understanding," but she sensed that the director expected her to nod.

"Yes," she said, "different dimensions."

"Just so," said Mr. Pope, smiling first at her and then at Dr. Novak. "But, though you and I will never pierce these strange dimensions, our own Dr. Novak has pioneered a method that allows us to pull back their strange veil. Just for the briefest instant, mind you–barely long enough to snap a photograph of the blushing universe behind."

"It's not a photograph," said Dr. Novak, "as I've explained to you a thousand times. A photograph would be useless. It's a holographic representation, which we can mine for further information."

Mr. Pope winked at Miss Smalls, as if to say: photograph, holograph–close enough between friends, no?

"Now the feat you have just heard is already a miracle of science, and would have been rewarded with a Nobel in a more enlightened age," said Mr. Pope, affecting not to notice as Dr. Novak muttered something about politics. "But for my money the real miracle is not the theory, but the application–what our staff can then do with these photographs that are not photographs. In the case of our mutual friend the

Governor, for example, they analyzed ... how many parallel universes was it, Dr. Novak?"

"Over 1,000,000."

"Over 1,000,000 parallel universes for evidence of two things: whether in each universe the governor had promised to support charter schools during his campaign, and whether he had won. Then, with the application of sophisticated statistical methods ... "

"Counting and some elementary t-tests," said Dr. Novak.

"... we were able to advise the governor that publicly supporting charter schools would certainly yield him at least a 3.6% edge in the election ... "

"That was with 90% confidence."

"... and he exploited this advice to his political advantage. Is that clear?"

"I'm missing something," said Miss Smalls. "You're saying you looked at these–parallel universes–to see the future of *our* universe?"

"Not to see our future, precisely," said Mr. Pope. "To make a more educated guess as to where the path of our future might lead."

"But why does it matter in this universe if something happens in a different one? I mean, in *Thymelines* the universes were totally separate–people could even die in one universe and be fine in the other."

"That's actually a very intelligent question," said Dr. Novak, and Mr. Pope smiled at him in approbation. "As I was trying to explain to you–before I was interrupted–there are an infinite number of *potential* parallel universes, but–for reasons we don't yet fully understand–not every potential universe actually exists. In fact, relatively speaking, the multiverse is shockingly sparse. But the universes that do exist aren't all equidistant to each other. They inhabit a Hilbert Space ... "

Mr. Pope clicked his tongue.

"... that is, what scientists like me call a 'Hilbert Space.' Some universes are–for lack of a better way to put it–closer to us than others, which means they resemble us more than others. Some of these are a little ahead of us in time, so if we look at enough of those universes–the ones that are close to us but ahead of us a little bit in time–we can count up different outcomes and make an educated guess about where we're headed as well."

"So," said Miss Smalls, "it's like if, in *Thymelines*, I had experienced one universe where I got up on the left side of the bed and died that day, and two universes where I got up on the right side and lived, it would be smarter for me to get up on the right side of the bed–because I'd be more likely to live?"

"Brava, Miss Smalls!" said Mr. Pope, actually standing and clapping his hands together once. "Brava indeed! You have no idea how few of our clients ever arrive at such a sophisticated level of understanding, let alone so quickly."

"You have no idea how few clients we even have," Dr. Novak said.

"All the better," said Mr. Pope, sitting again and gazing daggers at his partner, "to offer such highly individualized service."

"No, I definitely get it," said Miss Smalls. "It's actually really interesting. It could make a great film, if you could find a human element–a throughline for the story."

"It *is* interesting, I agree" Mr. Pope said. "But even more interesting than what we do, is what we can do *for you*–our very own human element, if you will. So, Miss Smalls: what has brought you to us today?"

"I've been offered a part," she said. "Back on the screen, not the stage. It's a great role–a young single mother, battling cancer and prejudice in her workplace. If I take this and nail it, it's my ticket back to the Hollywood A-list. No more supporting roles on Broadway–or off Broadway. It might even mean an Academy Award. I don't know if you realize how brutal Hollywood is, but an actress without at least a nomination by the time she's 30 doesn't get any more parts–ever. If I still want to be working in a few years, I need to be more than a body and a face–I need to be taken seriously as an actress, and I don't have a lot of time left. This could be my last chance."

"So far it sounds like congratulations and wishes of good fortune are in order, not advice," said Mr. Pope. "I assume there is a catch?"

"I'd have to shave my head for the role."

The room was silent for a moment–even Mr. Pope was at a loss.

"So?" said Dr. Novak finally.

"I'm not sure I want to shave my head."

"Then use one of those bald caps or whatever."

"No, I can't use a bald cap, because they want me to shave it on screen, in this very dramatic, realistic scene–it's the clip they'll show at the awards if I'm nominated. Maddie–the character I'd be playing–is supposed to be starting chemo the next day, but I *choose*

51

to cut off my own hair and face what's coming. I take control and don't let the cancer dictate what happens to me when."

"If you're shaving your head because you're about to begin chemo," said Dr. Novak, "it sounds to me like the cancer *is* dictating what happens to you and when."

"No one has ever accused Dr. Novak of an artistic sensibility," said Mr. Pope. "He is a man of facts, and does not lend much credit to the delicate tissue of truths between them. But vaster souls must learn to suffer those who are blind in their hearts, no? Furthermore, I can promise you"–this he delivered in a stage whisper, leaning away from Dr. Novak and towards Miss Smalls–"that when he sees your movie–and he will–he will suddenly find something in his eye during just that scene, and have to wipe away a few tears with his salt-and-butter-soaked napkin."

Dr. Novak's face turned red.

"Nevertheless, I must admit to sharing some of Dr. Novak's mystification at your dilemma," continued Mr. Pope. "Surely the shaving of your head is a small price to pay for such a role? Your hair is your trademark, I recognize, but surely that will only make the scene more powerful still. And it will grow back within, what, a year? Just in time to accept your golden statue with a new, flowing hairstyle."

"Of course it will grow back, it's just hair. But this isn't about vanity."

"Then what is it about?"

"I'm not sure I want to say," said Miss Smalls, glancing at Dr. Novak. "It's embarrassing–it's personal."

"Miss Smalls, we really cannot help you unless we understand your problem. We need positive and negative outcomes–like winning and losing the election for Governor Schwarzenegger–for our measurements. I assure you, once again, that everything you say in this room will stay in this room. The discretion of every employee of Educated Alternatives would be legendary–if we were not so discreet about it."

Miss Smalls sat for a few beats, until the silence became uncomfortable.

"Do you know who my husband is?" she said finally.

"I don't pretend to be an expert in the cinema, but it's difficult not to have heard of Ryan Bradley."

Dr. Novak reversed his angry slouch.

"Ryan Bradley is your husband?" he said. "*The* Ryan Bradley? Who directed *Fateful Moon*?"

"And *Night of the Platypus*, yes," said Miss Smalls. "And *Sunspots*, and *Points North*."

"Dr. Novak spends most of his time in the lab with his equations and computers," Mr. Pope said. "As you can see, he is a bit behind on his breaking culture news."

"We've been married for six years," said Miss Smalls.

"Perhaps more than a bit behind."

"But," said Dr. Novak, "his movies are so much …"

Mr. Pope commanded him with a look, and for once, Dr. Novak noticed and obeyed.

"… *different* than yours," he finished.

"You mean 'better.' No," she said, holding up her hand in Mr. Pope's direction, "don't jump on him for being honest–he's right. You're absolutely right. My husband's movies are worlds better than mine. If we were to retire right now–move out of LA, start the family we've talked about, spend more time with our charities–he would be remembered. In 20 years he'll be accepting a lifetime achievement award. 100 years from now people will still be watching *Points North*. But *Lingerie Lane*? *Red Hearts*? *Starfall*? Those won't even be on Netflix."

"*Starfall* might be on Netflix," said Dr. Novak. "There are some pretty good scenes between you and the alien. But if you can already be this honest with yourself, why are you even here? Take the part, shave your head, and go make better movies."

Miss Smalls uncrossed her legs and re-crossed them in Dr. Novak's direction. The scientist remained unaware of this social signal, but Mr. Pope noted it and reclined in his chair, crossing his hands on his gigantic belly with the pleased air of a director who has finally brokered peace between his warring leads.

"That's exactly what I want to do," she said. "My husband is more than an entertainer. He's become an actual artist–an artist of the screen. That's what I want, too, but I've never had that chance. I can't get the parts with any real meat to them, because this ..."

She swept her hand down along her body.

"... and this ..."

She circled her face with her finger.

"... and this ..."

She indicated the silk scarf on her head and what it covered.

" ... mean that I'm only allowed to play three parts: the bimbo, the slut, or–if I'm lucky–the perfect, unobtainable woman. Honestly, sometimes as I say the lines I'm given I can actually *feel* myself getting stupider."

"I get all that," said Dr. Novak. "But that's why I *don't* get why you're not just taking the part and shaving your head. I mean, by being so concerned about your own appearance, aren't you basically playing right along with their whole game? So what's the problem?"

Miss Smalls glanced almost askance at Mr. Pope where he still sat with his "my job is done here" attitude–as if he were now the one she wasn't quite sure about–before squaring her shoulders and leaning in towards Dr. Novak.

"Madame Rwanda told me that Ryan would leave me if I cut my hair," she said.

"Madame Rwanda?"

"She's my psychic."

Mr. Pope snapped out of his relaxed posture.

"You have a … psychic?" Dr. Novak said.

"She's not mine personally–I mean, a lot of us use her. She's amazing. She met Chano Pozo when she was just a little girl, right before he died. He's the one who told her she had the second sight. He even gave her the chicken bone he used to dowse–she still wears it around her neck."

"What the … " Dr. Novak began, but Mr. Pope cut him off.

"And you're confident in Madame Rwanda's predictions?"

"She's not one of those frauds, you should know that about her. She never claims to predict the future. She has visions, that's all. The way she explains it there are many different paths that the world can take, and they're all laid out for her, but dimly, until sometimes one lights up, like the lights on a runway at night–that's how she describes it. It's not that different than what you guys do, actually."

A bitter laugh from Dr. Novak.

"But she's right more than she's wrong," said Miss Smalls. "So I'm ... worried. And when I saw Arnie at his fundraiser, I asked him who he might talk to about something important–who *besides* Madame Rwanda–and he gave me your name."

"We'll have to send him a fruit and nut basket," said Dr. Novak.

"So you've come to us to get a second opinion," said Mr. Pope. "Very sensible. But I do have a question or two. What were the exact words that Madame Rwanda used? Sometimes these psychic predictions can be a bit open to interpretation–a bit ... "

"Fraudulent?" offered Dr. Novak.

"... oracular. Do you remember?"

"I'll never forget," said Miss Smalls. "I only asked her if I should take the role–I didn't even tell her the part about shaving my head. But I could tell from her reaction something was wrong–she threw the tarot three separate times. The last time she even used her own personal deck–I mean the one she keeps to ask her own questions–she never does that. She told me that she'd seen something, but she didn't understand what it meant, or how it answered my question. She didn't want to tell me what it was–I had to ask her a couple times–but finally she took my hand and said 'This is what I saw: your hair is what allows Ryan to love you.' "

"I see," said Mr. Pope. "I suppose that doesn't seem to allow for much interpretation."

"I can't believe I'm a party to this nonsense," said Dr. Novak.

"Dr. Novak, please," said Mr. Pope. "Our clients must reveal sensitive details of their lives in order for us to do our jobs–I must insist that you treat that with respect."

"This is bullshit. Look, Miss Smalls, I'm sorry for your troubles, and I'm sympathetic to the situation you find yourself in, career-wise. But let's call a spade a spade. Psychics aren't real–they're BS artists. Snake-oil salesmen who tell gullible people what they want to hear in order to part them from their money. Second of all, even if I were to stipulate that your 'Madame Rwanda' actually had some way to see the future–which I don't–then what we're basically saying here is that you're worried your husband only loves you for your hair. Now if that's what you actually think, then why do you care whether he stays or goes? Because it's good for your career to stay married to Ryan Bradley?"

"Dr. Novak!" said Mr. Pope, his face turning red.

"You think you know all about me," said Miss Smalls, pointing at the scientist, "and all about Hollywood marriages, and that our lives are shiny and shallow. But you don't know anything–not about me, or my husband, or our marriage. I love Ryan, and he loves me."

"Because of your hair?"

"Dr. Novak!" said Mr. Pope, standing up, "this has gone far enough. I dislike descending to threats, but I must remind you that I am still CEO of this enterprise, and that as such, I am your direct superior. Now I have nothing but respect for you and your brilliant mind, but if you wish to continue playing with your theories and machines–your very expensive machines, which this company pays for–I must insist that you control your tongue and treat our clients with respect."

Dr. Novak waved his hands and turned his face towards the wall.

"Miss Smalls," continued Mr. Pope, sitting and adjusting his lapels, "I apologize profoundly for that outburst. To the matter at hand: it's quite a conundrum you're faced with, but you have come to the right place. What our chief scientist lacks in common courtesy he makes up for in raw scientific skill, and we will apply all that skill to the dilemma in which you find yourself. We might not have the ... flair of a Madame Rwanda, and we might employ different methods, but I can promise you that our results will be no less accurate."

"Yes, that we can definitely promise," said Dr. Novak in a plausibly deniable whisper.

"It's not that I think Ryan could actually be so shallow, really," said Miss Smalls. "It's just ... I want to be sure."

"Miss Smalls, we have our positive and negative outcomes–there is no need to explain yourself further. Your marriage is your own business, and we are not here to judge ... "

He turned towards Dr. Novak as he said this.

"... but rather to educate you on the alternatives you wish to explore."

"All right," said Miss Smalls, though she looked less than entirely convinced. "All right. So what do we do from here?"

"Pretty simple, really," said Dr. Novak. "I'll just look deep into my crystal ball and drink some frog's blood and throw a chicken bone in the air and spin around three times at midnight–that's midnight Greenwich Mean Time, of course–and a friendly spirit will appear and tell me whether your husband will leave you if you shave your head."

Miss Smalls waved Mr. Pope off before he could answer.

"You think you're very clever," she said, "judging Madame Rwanda like that, but you shouldn't look down on her just because she's not a scientist or whatever. There are other ways to think about the world besides all your formulas and equations–maybe if you looked into them you'd lose some of that bitterness. At least Madame Rwanda helps people."

Dr. Novak scoffed.

"And at the *very* least," said Miss Smalls, "she knows how to treat a client. She understands that she's being asked to provide a service, not her own opinions on things. You could learn a thing or two there."

Mr. Pope laughed.

"Well spoken, Miss Smalls!" he said. "Well spoken indeed! Come, Dr. Novak, don't pout. The lady gives as good as she gets, and you must admit–you had it coming. This kind of spirited exchange is just how strong personalities become friends. Imagine if this were a movie, Miss Smalls–this little dust-up would have been your meet cute. Soon you and Dr. Novak would be as thick as thieves."

"I guess," said Miss Smalls.

"I feel quite sure," Mr. Pope said. "But now that we are all friends again, there is another topic we must broach–the vulgar topic of numbers ..."

"I don't care about that," said Miss Smalls. "Just bill it as 'Professional Coaching' and Ryan won't raise an eyebrow."

"You're positive? Dr. Novak's machines are not cheap to run."

"I'm sure."

"We are always delighted to hear that money is no object. When do you need your answer?"

"I have until Monday to accept the role."

Mr. Pope whistled.

"Is that impossible?" Miss Smalls asked.

Mr. Pope looked at Dr. Novak, who, still red and angry, nodded his head.

"Impossible? No," said Mr. Pope. Dr. Novak threw up his arms. "But difficult. And–I regret to say–even more expensive."

"Then bill it as 'Expedited Professional Coaching.' "

"Hold on," said Dr. Novak. "Look, I'm sorry if I was out of line, all right? Your marriage and psychics and all that are none of my business. But it doesn't matter how much we bill, or what we bill it as–there's no way we can get this done by Monday."

"Yet another challenge to which you will rise, astounding us all once again," Mr. Pope said.

"Goddamn it, I'm not joking–you can't go promising things we can't do. Just defining the feature matrix could take until Monday! Then there's the actual holographing, the automated filtering pass, the human filtering pass, the interpretive pass ..."

As the two men continued to argue, Miss Smalls reached up and, as if it had begun to bother her, undid the knot that held the silk scarf under her chin. She whisked the thin cloth sideways off her head.

Later, recalling the scene, Dr. Novak would have the impression that the sun had broken through the clouds at that precise moment; that the coffee he had been nursing had finally kicked his nervous system into gear; that the fans of the building's ancient ventilation system had been inspired at last to exchange the stale air of the conference room for some of the brisk autumnal atmosphere. At the time, however, he was aware of none of these things, being overwhelmed by a series of memories so sensory and varied that he could make no sense of them or their variety. He could hear the crack of bat against ball, and see the parabola intending towards the patch of grassy outfield that was his to guard. There was the patter of rain against the roof of the Braxton family's Chevrolet, and foggy windows through which he could just see the lonely riverbank where he and Julie Braxton had parked. He could sense the scent of steeping tea spiced for Christmas, and of cement after a rainstorm–and somewhere, beneath even those notes, the smell of his infant nephew's skin.

Such was the effect when Janine Smalls tossed her golden hair.

When he regained awareness of his surroundings, Dr. Novak saw that Mr. Pope–who was wiping his forehead with a pocket square–had not been immune either. It appeared that neither could remember what had happened to their argument, which now seemed trivial in light of what they had just witnessed together.

"All right," said Dr. Novak, and his very voice sounded foreign and unimportant to him. "We'll get you an answer by Monday."

Monday

When Miss Smalls returned on Monday morning the receptionist was prepared. She had been standing by the door since 6 o'clock, just in case, spinning and passing the doorman's umbrella from hand to hand to discharge some of her nervous energy, and as soon as she saw the car speeding down the access road she sprinted towards the already flooded parking lot, so that when Janine Smalls opened her car door she was greeted by the blue sky and puffy clouds painted on the underside of the umbrella and the receptionist's sunny smile. Not a single drop of rain even fell on her silk scarf.

After this promising beginning, however, and another sealed bottle of slightly cool Italian water, Miss Smalls found herself deposited in the same meeting room without even a hint of when Mr. Pope might be expected. Twice in the next ten minutes she considered storming out, but each time she checked the clock on her cell phone–her decision was expected within six hours–and decided to give Mr. Pope another five minutes. Once she thought she heard distant shouting and slamming of doors–or perhaps it had only been thunder.

When Mr. Pope finally arrived, all directorial authority was gone from his manner–he waited for her permission to enter after knocking, and as he shuffled into the room apology and shame fit him like a new vest and jacket. So Janine went where the scene took her.

"Our meeting was at 8," she said.

"I am so sorry to have made you wait, Miss Smalls ..."

"You didn't *make* me do anything. I *chose* to wait. I hope what you have for me is worth it."

Mr. Pope sat down, rubbing his hands together as if trying to scrub off any residue of responsibility.

"I find myself in the unique situation ..." he began. "That is to say, this has never happened here. Which is to say–in fact, there is no good way to say this. We have not been able to provide you with the level of service that you both expect and deserve."

"You're not done?" said Miss Smalls, ice forming on every word. "You know the schedule I'm on. How much longer will it be?"

"I'm afraid that time isn't the question here. We've had a–that is, there's been a glitch. A technical glitch. Is what I'm told."

"Then how long will it take to fix the glitch?"

"This particular glitch–I am told–cannot be fixed."

"A glitch is only a glitch if you can fix it. Look, I don't really care about any of this–I just want my answer. I need my answer. I have to call Maurice very, very soon."

"All I am able to offer you at this point are my profoundest apologies, my sincerest wishes that we have not inconvenienced you too much, and of course"–these words seemed to stick in his throat–"a full refund."

"Inconvenienced me? I was depending on you. This is a one-shot deal, Mr. Pope. Now I'll call Maurice and have him run interference, and you get back there and tell Dr. Novak to do whatever he has to do, fix whatever *glitches* he has to fix, and get me my answer. I don't care how he does it, just get it done."

Mr. Pope stood up.

"I'm afraid that's impossible, Miss Smalls–there's nothing more for Dr. Novak to do. If you will excuse me, I have some urgent matters that demand my attention. But if you have phone calls to make you are welcome, of course, to use the conference room for as long as you like–or at least until the electric company cuts service to the building."

He left the room over her amazed objections, swaying slightly.

Janine Smalls sat in the parked rental car, watching as fat drops of rain plowed down the windshield. Her phone lay on the passenger seat, silenced and blinking–Maurice was calling again.

"Get a hold of yourself," she said out loud. "It's just a role. It's just *one role*. There will be others. But on the other hand–it's just my hair. A year without hair. Can that really be all he loves? And if it is, do I even"–it took some effort to get the words out–"do I even *want* to stay married to him?"

And just like that, it was clear to her, as if illuminated by a flash of lightning. She had been in the wrong movie. This was not *Thymelines*–she was not choosing between her career and personal fulfillment. This was *Red Hearts*, and she was Sally, fleeing the truth by any means necessary, too blinded by love to allow herself to ask the question: had her husband only married her for her money? (Or–in Janine's present and even more ridiculous case–her hair?)

And considering that angle, was there even a choice? If Ryan's love was really contingent on her hair, on something physical, something so trivial, then–as hard as the possibility might be to countenance–it wasn't love at all.

"Enough," Janine Smalls said, picking up the phone. She began to dial.

Tap, tap, tap, sounded something to her left, and the window went dark. Janine Smalls screamed and stepped on the gas without thinking, but also without effect, as she had not yet started the car. Tap, tap, tap: a face, just visible through the streaks of rain.

"What the hell is wrong with you?" she shouted at Dr. Novak as she rolled the window down. "You scared me half to death."

"You can't take the part."

"I *am* taking the part. I've made up my mind–no thanks to you and your technical glitches."

"No, you *can't* take the part."

Miss Smalls took a moment to examine the scientist more carefully. He did not look quite right–which was to say, he looked even less right than the average person standing out in the rain without the apparent sense to get inside. His t-shirt and jeans were soaked through to his skin. His eyes did not seem to be focusing well, and dark crescents cupped them. There was something wild in his gaze.

"Are you all right, Dr. Novak?"

"You can't take the part. I have to *tell* you something."

Something in his manner made her suddenly and uncomfortably aware of how alone they were out in the parking lot.

"All right," she said, "why don't we go inside and you can tell me whatever you want."

"I can't go back in there–he'll kill me."

"No one's going to kill you."

"There are these monks somewhere in the mountains of Tibet–I think it's Tibet, I saw it on the History Channel, but it was so long ago, and at the time I just thought it was amusing. The monks shave their heads, all but one of them."

"Why don't you get in the car, at least?"

"They believe that he–the one monk who doesn't shave his head–is a reincarnation of one of their gods, an unconscious reincarnation–and his hair–his hair is sacred. It's like the thread holding everything together, and if he shaves it, or even cuts it too much, the universe will end. Just–blink out. So when he gets old and dies, the other monks have to go searching for his next reincarnation and bring him back to the monastery, where they can make sure he leaves his hair alone, because if they don't find him in time ... And since the last guy died they haven't been able to find his reincarnation–they've been searching for almost 30 years. I wonder whether they've ever even considered that they should be searching for a woman."

"That's fascinating, Dr. Novak. I'm going to call Mr. Pope so he can come get you in out of the rain."

"No!" shouted Dr. Novak, so loudly that she dropped the phone. "He'll kill me. He showed me the gun."

"Mr. Pope doesn't have a gun," Miss Smalls said, but she sounded even less sure than she felt.

"He keeps one in his office–ever since he took money from the Russians. Do you understand?"

"Which Russians?"

"No, do you understand about the monks?"

"Yes," she lied. "What if I call someone else? Not Mr. Pope, but some family, or a friend? I think you need some help."

"I searched trillions of universes. We've never looked at so many. I ran the machines for five days straight–you have no idea what that costs. I've bankrupted our company, Miss Smalls. It's the same in every universe. Do you understand?"

"I don't understand–you've ... bankrupted your company in every universe?"

"At first I was sure that it must be a mistake. But I checked every possible error condition–I cross-checked everything six ways to Sunday. There was no mistake. It was the same."

"Dr. Novak, what are you talking about? What was the same?"

"Your hair, Miss Smalls. Across every single one of those trillions of universes, bearing every variation imaginable, your hair was exactly the same. Just like this." For a second Miss Smalls thought he would reach through the window and touch it, and she bristled. "There should be millions of universes where you're a brunette. Millions where you're a redhead. Millions where you wear your hair short. Even some where you've already shaved it for a role. There are none. Zero. Do you understand? About the monks?"

"Dr. Novak, you're not making sense."

"I think Miss Rwanda was being *literal*. Your hair *allows* your husband to love you because it *allows* ... this is madness, I can't believe I'm saying this, thinking this. But that's why there are so few parallel universes, when we should see so many, because if you change your hair too much in any given universe ... That is–Miss Smalls–" said Dr. Novak, straightening his posture somewhat, "it is my scientific opinion that, for the sake of your career, your marriage, and ... many, many other things ... you should not accept this role, or any role that requires you to shave, dye, or otherwise alter your hair to any significant degree."

He stood for a moment, searching for something else to say.

"I'm sorry," was all he managed.

He turned and walked away, the water sloshing around his ankles with every step.

"Dr. Novak!"

The scientist turned around as Miss Smalls dug through her wallet.

"Take this," she said, holding a business card out the window. Dr. Novak walked back to retrieve it. "To help you figure out what's next. Tell Miss Rwanda I sent you."

Dr. Novak looked at the card, then at Miss Smalls, then at the card again.

"Thank you," he said, and put it in his pocket.

Tuesday

"You smell like cigarettes," said Janine Smalls.

"There was a lot of second-hand smoke at the party," Ryan Bradley said, stooping to kiss his wife on the head. He sat down in the recliner adjoining the sofa where she lay stretched out.

"You also smell like alcohol."

"Lots of second-hand scotch too. Are we reading parts?"

"If you want to call them that," said Janine, tossing another screenplay onto a pile on the floor and taking the next from the stack on which she had propped up her feet. "I swear to you, I don't know why I pay Maurice to find me this garbage."

"If I had an Oscar for every time you threatened to fire Maurice ... "

"You *do* have an Oscar for every time I've threatened to fire Maurice."

"Heh, I suppose I do. What's wrong with this one?" said Ryan, picking up the screenplay she had just discarded and flipping open the light blue cover. *"Family Matters?"*

"She's a bitch, that's what wrong with it. A working mom who, in the first ten pages, manages to yell at her husband, her kids, and the hot young intern working for her. With whom she later has an affair. No one will root for her."

"Well that's all in how you play it, isn't it? You have to make the audience feel just how much depends on her–just how much weight is on her shoulders. What do you think about Luigi's for dinner? I'm in the mood for a bistec florentino."

"I had Sandy come by earlier, there are grilled vegetables with an arugula chimichurri on the counter and an egg white omelet in the fridge. Don't give me the face, I saw your latest test results–if cholesterol numbers were electoral votes you would be the next president. Speaking of which, Marcy told me the DNC called–they want you to direct something for them."

"No thanks."

"Don't tell me, tell Marcy."

"How about this one? *Scarlet Ambition*? I like the title. And it opens nice."

"It's sci-fi. I seem to remember a famous director advising me to stay out of sci-fi. Also, the heroine gets naked within the first ten minutes–which I seem to recall some more advice about. Furthermore she has the line 'It's quiet. Too quiet.' "

"You're kidding."

"Nope–it's on page four, about halfway down. And then, just to top it all off," said Janine Smalls, tossing another screenplay on a pile and turning to her husband, "she's a ginger."

Slices of Pi

From Mariposa Media Conglomerate v. Partensky

Roy Selva, Witness for the Plaintiff
Ulysses J. Fleetwell, Attorney for the Plaintiff
George Baniff, Attorney for the Defense

Selva: March 14th of last year? Yeah, I had contact with Igor–Mr. Partensky–that day.

Fleetwell: How did this contact come about?

Selva: I called him into my office that morning, before he went out on his calls.

Fleetwell: You were his direct superior at the time?

Selva: That's right, I manage all the field technicians in Mariposa's Boston office.

Fleetwell: And at that time Mr. Partensky was a field technician in the employ of Mariposa Media Conglomerate?

Selva: His official title was "Field Technician, Class III."

Fleetwell: Can you describe the discussion that took place in your office on the morning of March 14th?

Selva: When Igor–I mean Mr. Partensky–came in he was a hot mess–sweating, shivering, and he smelled like he'd already been hitting the liquid courage. As soon as he saw that I was holding his "Equip Yourself!" application, he crumbled. He dropped to his knees, right there in front of my desk, and crossed himself like he was kneeling in front of an altar or something, and then started stabbing himself in the chest with his hands over and over, like he was holding a knife. He was praying–sometimes in English, sometimes in Russian. Just a mess. My heart just went out to the guy. Anyone's would have.

Fleetwell: What was the "Equip Yourself!" program?

Selva: That was a pilot program for the field techs to buy their own equipment. Mariposa would reimburse them up to 90%.

Fleetwell: Why would field technicians want to buy their own equipment?

Selva: Maybe, you know, one of them preferred a different brand of voltmeter, or a wire-stripper with a handle especially contoured for lefties. The company thought it would be a nice perk to give them a little flexibility.

Fleetwell: So Mr. Partensky had applied to participate in the "Equip Yourself!" program?

Selva: Yeah.

Fleetwell: By submitting an application for reimbursement to you, his direct superior?

Selva: That's right.

Fleetwell: Had he bought his own voltmeter, of the special brand he preferred?

Selva: No.

Fleetwell: His own left-handed wire-stripper, then?

Selva: No.

Fleetwell: Then what had Mr. Partensky bought and submitted for reimbursement under the "Equip Yourself!" program?

Selva: A laptop.

Fleetwell: Do you happen to recall the make and model of this laptop?

Selva: It was a Toshiba Q100.

Fleetwell: Was there anything noteworthy about that particular make and model?

Selva: Yeah, it was the first–I guess you'd call it "consumer" machine–to ship with a quantum coprocessor.

Fleetwell: A "quantum coprocessor?" That sounds expensive.

Selva: It was.

Fleetwell: How expensive?

Selva: $23,000 and change.

Fleetwell: Which was the amount for which Mr. Partensky was seeking reimbursement?

Selva: He was asking for 90%, which was the maximum allowed under the program. So a little over $20,000.

Fleetwell: What was the amount of the average reimbursement request for the "Equip Yourself!" program?

Selva: I don't really have those numbers off the top of my head.

Fleetwell: Ballpark–to, say, the nearest $1,000.

Selva: Oh, that's easy–all the other requests were way under $1,000.

Fleetwell: You mean that every other reimbursement request you received in the Boston office under the "Equip Yourself!" program was under $1,000?

Selva: Yeah, they were all maybe $50 or $100 at the most.

Fleetwell: Can you describe briefly the duties that a Field Technician, Class III is expected to perform for Mariposa Media Conglomerate?

Selva: Um, sure. The Class IIIs handle mostly the same stuff as the Class I and IIs–installations, basic repairs–but they also get called in for the really tough problems.

Fleetwell: What are the really tough problems?

Selva: Maybe a customer is getting a bad picture, or the sound is still out of phase, even after we've swapped the box out a couple times, and the Class III might have to figure out why the network was misbehaving, or if there's a bad stretch of cable that needs to be tracked down, or if there's phase interference. That sort of thing.

Fleetwell: That all sounds pretty complicated.

Selva: It can be.

Fleetwell: And which problems were made easier for Mr. Partensky to solve, in his capacity as a Field Technician, Class III, by the purchase of his new Q100 laptop with its quantum coprocessor?

Selva: Well–it's honestly hard to see how a quantum coprocessor would have helped him much.

Fleetwell: Much?

Selva: At all.

Fleetwell: Would it be fair to say that you, as an expert on the duties and responsibilities of Field Technicians, Class III, would be unable to conceive of even a hypothetical use that a Field Technician, Class III might have for a quantum coprocessor in the execution of his duties?

Selva: Yeah, I guess. I mean, if there is a use, I can't think of it.

Fleetwell: So why had Mr. Partensky submitted the laptop for reimbursement?

Baniff: Objection: calls for speculation.

Fleetwell: I'll rephrase: on the morning of March 14th of last year, in your office, did Mr. Partensky tell you why he had submitted the Toshiba Q100 laptop for reimbursement?

Selva: Yes, he said that he'd–well, made a mistake.

Fleetwell: Was that how he phrased it to you?

Selva: No, in his words, he'd "fucked up." "I fucked up," he kept saying. "I know I fucked up."

Fleetwell: Can you elaborate?

Selva: He said he'd bought the laptop in a "moment of weakness," even though he knew he couldn't afford it. He'd emptied his checking and maxed out his credit card–he wasn't even going to be able to make rent that month, or send his daughter to camp like he'd promised.

Fleetwell: So he thought to try to apply for reimbursement through the "Equip Yourself!" program–even though he hadn't bought the laptop for the purpose of his duties at Mariposa Media Conglomerate?

Selva: That's right.

Fleetwell: Did he say what purpose he had bought it for?

Selva: He mentioned something about finishing his dissertation, and information theory–honestly I couldn't follow it very well, he was very upset, and a lot of it was pretty technical.

Fleetwell: But you're very technical, aren't you?

Selva: This was a different kind of technical–not cable television and internet stuff–more like stuff he'd been working on when he was going after his PhD.

Fleetwell: And on this occasion, on March 14th, did Mr. Partensky ask you for anything?

Selva: He asked me to help him get reimbursed for the laptop, so that his wife ...

Fleetwell: So that his wife what, Mr. Selva?

Selva: So that his wife ...

Fleetwell: I know that the former Mrs. Partensky is a sensitive topic for you, Mr. Selva, but this is a court of law, convened to determine the facts surrounding a matter of intellectual property. Any personal indiscretions that may or may not have occurred by the wayside are simply irrelevant. Now, why did Mr. Partensky want your help to get reimbursed for the laptop?

Selva: He was afraid that his wife would leave him if she found out what he'd done.

Fleetwell: Thank you. Did Mr. Partensky say why he didn't just return the laptop?

Selva: I guess the cover had gotten all banged up when he threw it in the back of his truck, and the store wouldn't take it back. He said reimbursement was his only chance, and he really needed my help.

Fleetwell: So did you agree to help him? Mr. Selva?

Selva: Well, yeah. Yeah, of course I did. He was my best field tech. But apart from that, you would have done the same–anyone would have. He was just so broken, kneeling there on the floor, crying and praying and hitting himself in the chest. My heart just went out to the guy. I told him we'd work it out.

Fleetwell: How would you work it out?

Selva: I told him to take the day off, go home and rest, and that I would try to find something for him to do with the laptop that would let me slip it through and get him reimbursed.

Fleetwell: So your plan was to make reimbursement pos-sible by finding him some task that both legitimately served the interests of Mariposa Media Conglomerate and also legit-imately required a quantum coprocessor?

Selva: To be honest, I wasn't really thinking much about whether the task was a "legitimate" use of a quantum coprocessor or not. It just had to look good on paper.

Fleetwell: But, to be clear, you were specifically looking for a task–whether that task would have been, in your opin-ion, a "legitimate" use of a quantum coprocessor or not–that would fall within the purview of Mariposa Media Conglom-erate's legitimate, day-to-day business?

Selva: Yeah, of course, it would have to be for Mariposa–otherwise how was I going to argue that he should be reimbursed for the laptop? Look, I had no idea it was going to blow up like this–I never in a million years would have thought we'd end up here. I thought we were just talking about 20,000 dollars.

Fleetwell: And did you find such a task?

From *My 12 Memorable Cases (A Memoir)*, by Ulysses J. Fleetwell (un-published)

"Intellectual property."

No pair of words I ever managed to coax or compel together in my second career as New York's Poet Laureate has surpassed the tense energy that names the concern of my first.

Even today, here in the gray backwaters of retirement, I roll them on my tongue and they conjure up an image for me: a sun god gazing down with stern approval as a horde of intellectual property attorneys, invisible but for the merest perturbation of the atmosphere, like angels bear the sun-god's gifts from Heaven to Earth. In my day I was one of these beasts of subtle burden–an intellectual property lawyer–and it is matter of public record rather than boast when I note that I had one of the widest backs.

[...]

No doubt you have benefited from my work, gentle reader, though no doubt you did so unawares. The Klauser Touchless Faucet that allows you to wash your hands in the office sink without picking up the germs left by your colleagues with their questionable hygiene; the S84-E engine, which set a new standard for power and fuel efficiency, bringing down the price of minivans sufficiently that you and your spouse could shuttle your 2.5 children in comfort and safety around the leafy suburb you call home; the Philips Juvenile Bile Duct Stent, which may have saved the life of one of your nieces or nephews afflicted by pancreatitis–I represented the inventors of all these against an onslaught of cranks, opportunists, and pretenders. And even if you have somehow dodged all my aforementioned handiwork, it is almost unthinkable that you have not enjoyed the results of my most famous suit, Mariposa Media Conglomerate v. Partensky.

Last night, gentle reader, I suspect you passed the time before bed enjoying a recorded entertainment–perhaps a period romance or some absurdly inaccurate courtroom drama. Unless there happened to be a rare malfunction, I doubt you gave any thought whatsoever to how that recorded entertainment actually entered your home–what role the wires running to your bedroom played, or the large cable box to the side of your television, which grows warm while you enjoy your sitcom. If you are not old enough to remember, then surely your parents are, a time when the cable box was much smaller–small enough to fit in the palm of your hand–and the monthly cable bill was much, much larger–obscenely large, when you consider that in those days the selection of recorded entertainment consisted only of what happened to be playing at that moment on one of the various "channels"–rather than the instant access we enjoy today to every movie and every episode of every show ever made.

[...]

It is easy to take such developments for granted. Thus proceeds the march of progress, one thinks–the anonymous and inevitable march of progress. But witnessed from the trenches, the "march of progress" is anything but inevitable, and barely a march–on many days it seems little more than a desperate stumble.

[...]

As the tree of liberty requires occasional refreshment by the blood of patriots, so the tree of progress withers and dies unless it basks continually in the rays of intellectual property law.

[...]

Partensky took the job at Mariposa, abandoning an unfinished degree in mathematics, when his wife Laurie became pregnant. I could find no evidence of his ever having complained about the position, though it was far beneath his intellectual capabilities. Likewise there is no record of his ever having agitated for a transfer or promotion. Day after day for seven years he put on his Mariposa vest and drove the company van around the greater Boston area, installing and repairing cable connections for the local subscribers, and neither his customers or co-workers ever suspected the intellect and advanced training he was wasting in the process. He was either one of those men without ambitions beyond the demands of the moment, or one whose ambitions are so large and unusual that they cannot be defined or perhaps even understood in the customary social structures.

[...]

Igor Partensky was the underdog in Mariposa Media Conglomerate v. Partensky, the David to Mariposa's Goliath. It feels just and right to root for the underdog, and nearly inhuman to root for a "conglomerate"–and all the more so because the underdog in this case was such a character, and such a sympathetic one. In the interviews I conducted, Partensky's co-workers describe a cheerful bear of a man, forever slapping backs and laughing with his mouth full. His customer reviews are almost uniformly excellent, praising both his expertise and good nature–his lone one-star review coming from a Baptist preacher to whom Partensky apparently offered a swig of vodka from a mayonnaise jar.

Yes, Igor Partensky was an interesting, likable fellow, and an undeniable genius to boot–and it would be all too easy to see him as the hero, or perhaps the victim. But nothing could be further from the truth. Igor Partensky is the villain in this tale, the spreading shadow hoping to prevent the sun god's gifts from arriving to the earth–the spiteful demon gnawing at the very root of the tree of progress.

From Mariposa Media Conglomerate v. Partensky

Jane Smiley, Witness for the Plaintiff
Ulysses J. Fleetwell, Attorney for the Plaintiff

Fleetwell: Ms. Smiley, did you know Igor Partensky during his employment at Mariposa Media Conglomerate?

Smiley: I knew his name, certainly–I always had to chase him down on email about his vacations. Field techs are supposed to report their vacation two weeks in advance, and he never would. Sometimes he would actually submit his vacation *after* he was actually ...

Fleetwell: But did you ever meet the man himself?

Smiley: Yes, but only once as far as I recall, when he and Roy Selva came into my office one morning.

Fleetwell: Was that the morning of April 2nd of last year?

Smiley: That's right.

Fleetwell: And what is your title at Mariposa Media Conglomerate?

Smiley: I'm the Special Manager in Charge of Field Technician Scheduling in the Boston office.

Fleetwell: Can you briefly describe the function you serve in that role?

Smiley: Just like it sounds, I'm in charge of the group that schedules the Field Technicians. We schedule installations and dispatch service calls.

Fleetwell: What happened when Mr. Partensky and Mr. Selva came into your office that morning?

Smiley: It was rather confusing. He kept talking about scheduling and traveling salesmen–but we don't handle sales, that's a whole different department. He was going a mile a minute–it was very overwhelming.

Fleetwell: For the record, whose behavior are you describing? Mr. Selva's or Mr. Partensky's?

Smiley: Mr. Partensky's. He kept holding his laptop out in front of him like this, like he was offering me a cigar from a box, and he kept wanting me to look at the screen. He was very insistent.

Fleetwell: Did you look at what he had on the laptop?

Smiley: I tried to, it was hard to understand.

Fleetwell: What was on the screen?

Smiley: Just a bunch of numbers. The font was very small.

Fleetwell: What did you say to Mr. Partensky?

Smiley: Mostly I just nodded and smiled. He was very friendly, just very–excitable, and I couldn't understand what he was saying. Then he erased my whiteboard, without even asking, and started drawing on it. I had important work on that whiteboard–I keep the vacation scheduling there.

Fleetwell: What did Mr. Partensky draw, do you remember?

Smiley: A lot of circles and arrows. He talked a lot about graphs, I remember that, but I don't think he ever actually drew any graphs. I really didn't understand what he was getting at, and I was upset that he'd erased the vacations.

Fleetwell: How about Mr. Selva? Did he say anything to you?

Smiley: Yes, he wanted to know if I would be willing to reimburse Mr. Partensky's laptop from my department's budget.

Fleetwell: Did he say why he thought you might want to do that?

Smiley: He said that the stuff Mr. Partensky had been working on–with the numbers on the screen and so on–was a new way to schedule the field technician calls. A better way.

Fleetwell: What did you tell him?

Smiley: I told him that I didn't really understand, and that I had a meeting to run to, but that I would call him later that morning to discuss the matter. Honestly I didn't have a meeting, I was just a little overwhelmed by the whole experience and I wanted my office back to myself so I could redo the schedule he'd ruined on my whiteboard.

Fleetwell: Did you call Mr. Selva later?

Smiley: Yes, I did.

Fleetwell: What did you say to Mr. Selva on that phone call?

Smiley: Well ... to be honest, I was a little miffed, and I told him so. I said that I had found the whole visit very confusing and overwhelming, and that we already had scheduling software that worked just fine, and that I didn't understand why he wanted *me* to pay for a laptop for one of *his* field techs. Oh, and I suggested that if Mr. Partensky was interested in traveling salesmen, Mr. Selva should bring him to talk to sales.

Fleetwell: What did Mr. Selva say?

Smiley: He apologized and promised that he wouldn't bother me again about the matter.

From Mariposa Media Conglomerate v. Partensky

Alan Lightfoot, Witness for the Plaintiff
Ulysses J. Fleetwell, Attorney for the Plaintiff

Lightfoot: My title is Principal Research Scientist.

Fleetwell: During his employment at Mariposa Media Conglomerate did you ever meet Igor Partensky?

Lightfoot: Yes.

Fleetwell: Can you describe the circumstances in which you met him?

Lightfoot: He came into the research area one morning to show us some work he'd done.

Fleetwell: This was on April 15th of last year?

Lightfoot: That's right.

Fleetwell: What did he show you?

Lightfoot: It was a clip of "Steamboat Willie," playing in a loop on his laptop.

Fleetwell: Steamboat Willie?

Lightfoot: That's the original Mickey Mouse cartoon–Mickey Mouse standing on the deck of a steamboat, piloting it and whistling and, I don't know, doing his thing.

Fleetwell: Did you notice anything unusual about the clip?

Lightfoot: The colors were wrong. The original was black and white, but the clip was more like green and yellow, and there were splotches of other colors that came and went, like it was from a badly deteriorated print.

Fleetwell: Were you impressed with the clip that Mr. Partensky showed you?

Lightfoot: No. I mean not at first. At first I was worried that he might be crazy. He was kind of crooning to the laptop and talking a mile a minute.

Fleetwell: Do you remember anything in particular that he said?

Lightfoot: I remember he kept saying "Piece of cake, slice of pie!" and laughing as if it were the funniest thing in the world. That's the kind of stuff that made me think about calling security. But then he mentioned something about Kolmogorov numbers, and some other things that made a little sense, and that caught my attention. I started listening a little more carefully, and I started to think maybe he wasn't crazy–just scatterbrained, or really excited. That's about when the phone rang.

Fleetwell: Who was it?

Lightfoot: It was Roy Selva, from Field Operations. He told me he was sending down one of his guys to show me something–a field tech who happened to have some training in advanced mathematics–and asked if I'd take a few minutes to look at what Mr. Partensky was working on and then call him back with my thoughts. I told him that the field tech had already arrived. He warned me that Mr. Partensky was–in his words–a "live wire but a sweetheart." So that cleared things up a bit.

Fleetwell: What did you do then?

Lightfoot: I sat Mr. Partensky down and asked him to explain to me, slowly and calmly, what he'd been working on.

Fleetwell: Can you summarize the nature of what he told you?

Lightfoot: It took a while to get him to walk me through it–he was really all over the place–but what he described to me was an algorithm for the compression of data–specifically audio and video data.

Fleetwell: Was this what is known today as the "Slices of Pi" algorithm?

Lightfoot: That's right, in its basic, earliest form. It works by ...

Fleetwell: We'll have time to get into the gory details, Mr. Lightfoot. For the moment: what was your reaction to this work when Mr. Partensky described it to you?

Lightfoot: My reaction?

Fleetwell: Did it have applications to the business of Mariposa Media Conglomerate?

Lightfoot: Yeah, you could say that–if you wanted to win the award for understatement of the century.

Fleetwell: Can you elaborate?

Lightfoot: What Mr. Partensky showed me did an end run around the Shannon limit–at least theoretically–by ...

Fleetwell: In layman's terms, please, Mr. Lightfoot, and focusing on the impact on Mariposa Media Conglomerate's business?

Lightfoot: Right, sorry. Um, OK–basically he had found a way that we could push the same amount of data to our customers–the same movies, shows, music, etc.–and spend less money doing it. And he'd made a little proof of concept to show that it could actually work.

Fleetwell: Using "Steamboat Willie" as his example?

Lightfoot: That's right, he'd compressed "Steamboat Willie" using his algorithm.

Fleetwell: Can you roughly quantify the effect that Mr. Partensky's work might have on Mariposa Media Conglomerate's business?

Lightfoot: Sure, let me put it this way, I guess: it could change the fundamental economics of the business.

I mean, this is all a few years away from being practical–the prices of quantum coprocessors have to drop to commodity levels before we can start installing them in customer's homes, but that's just a matter of time. And then the impact will be enormous.

Fleetwell: Can you give a ballpark number?

Lightfoot: Tens of millions of dollars a year, at the very least. Maybe hundreds. And the impact won't be just on Mariposa's business–there's a tremendous range of other potential applications. Software updates, satellite communications. It's hard to overstate the breakthrough that Mr. Partensky's work might represent. It's ... revolutionary is really the only word for it. We don't really know yet just how far it will go.

Fleetwell: Did Mr. Partensky seem to understand the potential impact of his work? Did I say something funny, Mr. Lightfoot?

Lightfoot: I'm sorry, it's just ... I don't know how to answer that. He must have understood the potential applications–I mean, he's clearly a genius–but he didn't want to hear any of it. He just sat there drinking something from a jar–I think it was vodka–and laughing at us.

Fleetwell: Can you elaborate?

Lightfoot: While we were throwing out all these different applications–by this time I'd called in a bunch of the other research scientists, and we were all going crazy over this thing he'd done–Mr. Partensky basically sat in the corner of my office and made fun of us for getting so excited.

Fleetwell: Why would he make fun of you for being excited about his own work?

Lightfoot: He thought it was a toy.

Fleetwell: Did he use that term?

Lightfoot: Yes, he said it many times: "It's just a toy. A child's toy."

Fleetwell: Did he explain why he felt that way?

Lightfoot: Yes, he did.

Fleetwell: Can you summarize his argument? In layman's terms?

Lightfoot: Right, layman's terms. Basically his work made an assumption: that pi is what's called a "normal number." Now most people believe it is, but no one has ever been able to prove it. So yes, from a purely theoretical standpoint, you couldn't *prove* that his idea would always work.

Fleetwell: So his work would not be valuable if it turned out that pi wasn't actually a ... what was that term again?

Lightfoot: Normal number. No, it wasn't even that serious: if pi turned out not to be a normal number, then it just would have meant that *in theory* there might be videos that his algorithm couldn't encode. That's all. But it clearly worked–he'd already used it on "Steamboat Willie."

Fleetwell: For the layman, please, Mr. Lightfoot: are you saying Mr. Partensky's work would still have represented roughly the same financial benefit to Mariposa Media Conglomerate, even if pi turned out not to be a normal number?

Lightfoot: Sorry, yes. It really wouldn't have made much of a difference to the real-world application. It was still this huge real-world achievement, with huge potential applications and financial impact.

Here, maybe an analogy would help. Imagine that we couldn't *prove* that airplanes *should* be able to fly. As a basic, everyday traveler, if you see them taking off and landing every day, do you really care? They obviously can fly–at least in normal conditions.

But I guess that just wasn't how Mr. Partensky saw it. He was taking a more theoretical or academic approach. He seemed to think that if you couldn't prove that his approach would always work, in all cases, then it didn't really amount to much more than a parlor trick.

Fleetwell: How did you leave things with Mr. Partensky that day?

Lightfoot: He gave us a copy of the source for the software he'd created, his proof of concept, and left–to go out on his field calls, I assume. He was still laughing at us on his way out the door.

Fleetwell: Did you call Mr. Selva back after Mr. Partensky left?

Lightfoot: Yes, I did.

Fleetwell: Did you tell him what you'd determined regarding Mr. Partensky's work? The potential impact? The larger implications?

Lightfoot: Yes, I did.

Fleetwell: And what did Mr. Selva have to say?

Lightfoot: He didn't really seem all that interested in the applications and impact and all that–he just wanted to know if my department would reimburse Mr. Partensky for 90% of the cost of the Q100 laptop he'd bought, based on the work he'd shown me.

Fleetwell: What was your answer?

Lightfoot: I told him we'd gladly reimburse Mr. Partensky the full 100% of the laptop–we'd have a check cut that same day, if he wanted.

Fleetwell: Did you call anyone else that morning?

Lightfoot: Yes.

Fleetwell: Who?

Lightfoot: Samuel Siskind–our corporate counsel here in New York.

Fleetwell: And what did you say to Mr. Siskind?

Lightfoot: I told him he needed to get on a plane and come talk to Mr. Partensky immediately.

Canceled Check (Plaintiff Exhibit C, Mariposa Media Conglomerate v. Partensky)

Not valid in amounts over $10,000 without two authorized signatures

Pay to the Order of: Igor Partensky

Amount: Twenty-three thousand two hundred and eleven dollars and 12/100ths

Signed: Janet Toth, Controller, Mariposa Media Conglomerate

Signed: Alexander Downs, CFO, Mariposa Media Conglomerate

Memo: Reimbursement #1432990

From *Slices of Pi for Total Morons*

So, you want to learn about Slices of Pi?

First of all, **congratulations!** You're about to embark on a journey of discovery through one of the biggest technological breakthroughs of the 21st Century!

Second of all, if you're **nervous** that we're going to throw a bunch of equations and formulas at you, **don't be**! We'll keep it simple, and take it in small steps. After all, that's the Moron way!

What is Slices of Pi?

Slices of pi is a **compression algorithm** originally designed by Igor Partensky, and now in wide use in many areas and industries.

(Fun fact: Igor Partensky was just a field technician who installed cable boxes for a living when he had the idea for Slices of Pi–and Einstein was working as a patent clerk when he came up with the theory of relativity!)

OK, Well Then What's a Compression Algorithm?

Don't get scared by the big-sounding words: it's pretty simple. "Compression" means taking data and making it smaller. And an "algorithm" is just a series of steps for doing something.

So when you read "compression algorithm" you can think "a **series of steps** for making **data smaller**."

It's just that simple!

Why Do We Want Smaller Data, Anyway?

Smaller data means you can fit **more photos and songs** on your hard drive.

Smaller data means that downloads finish **quicker**.

Smaller data means your cable company can offer you a **wider selection** of recorded entertainment–at a **lower price!**

In other words: when it comes to data, small is beautiful!

From Mariposa Media Conglomerate v. Partensky

Roy Selva, Witness for the Plaintiff
Ulysses J. Fleetwell, Attorney for the Plaintiff
The Honorable Marcus Whitney Bulger, Judge

Fleetwell: Mr. Selva, can you summarize the nature of the new contract that Mr. Siskind asked you to present to Mr. Partensky?

Selva: Sure. It pretty much said that he'd be promoted to Principal Research Scientist, with a big raise and so on, and that he'd acknowledge that he invented Slices of Pi on behalf of Mariposa Media Conglomerate.

Fleetwell: Did Mr. Siskind explain why he was asking you to present the contract to Mr. Partensky, rather than, say, presenting it himself?

Selva: Yeah, he said he thought it'd be better coming from a friend. That is, from someone that Mr. Partensky already knew.

Fleetwell: And did you present this contract to Mr. Partensky for his consideration?

Selva: I did.

Fleetwell: Would you describe his reaction to the contract as hostile? Aggressive? Wronged?

Selva: No, not at all–actually he seemed very happy with the idea. In fact he wanted to sign it right there and then–I had to stop him. I told him to take it home over the weekend and talk to his wife, at least.

Fleetwell: Might you have described him as grateful, even?

Selva: Yes, I guess you could say he seemed grateful. I mean, he was definitely grateful for getting the laptop reimbursed. That was what he kept mentioning–he seemed much more interested in that than in the contract.

Fleetwell: Did he express his gratitude to you in any concrete way? Mr. Selva?

Judge Bulger: The witness will please answer the question.

Notes on Napkin (Laurie Partensky's Handwriting)

(sunday dinner with Igor's boss!!)
lamb
potatoes (butter at home–cream?)
spinach
wine (look up what is a good one–red with lamb?)
desert?
hair??
new dress???

From *Slices of Pi for Total Morons*

How Does Slices of Pi Compress Data?

One of the interesting things about Slices of Pi is that it doesn't work the same way as normal compression algorithms do.

OK, How Do Normal Compression Algorithms Work?

Most compression algorithms look for **patterns** in data and use those patterns to make the data smaller.

For example, imagine our data was a number like this:

8888888888	8888888888	8888888888
8888888888	8888888888	8888888888
8888888888		

That's a lot of 8s! In fact, if you count, you'll find that's **70** of them!

A normal compression algorithm facing this data would say something like "Hmm, I'm noticing a lot of 8s in here," and compress it to something like:

Write 70 8s

That's a lot smaller, right? Way to go, normal compression algorithm!

Putting Our Normal Compression Algorithm through Its Paces

Let's say we tacked another 8 on to the end of our data, so now we had **71**, like so:

8888888888 8888888888 8888888888
8888888888 8888888888 8888888888
88888888888

Our normal compression algorithm wouldn't even break a sweat dealing with the extra 8. Instead of:

Write 70 8s

... it would just compress the data to:

Write 71 8s

So the compressed version of our new data–with 71 8s–would be just as small as the compressed version of our old data–with only 70 8s. Even if we added 100 more 8s, the compressed version of our data wouldn't grow much:

Write 170 8s

Neat!

But what would happen if we added a **1** instead of an **8**, so our data looked like this?

8888888888 8888888888 8888888888
8888888888 8888888888 8888888888
88888888881

Now our normal compression algorithm would have to compress it to something like:

Write 70 8s and 1 1

Wow! The compressed version of our data just got a lot **bigger**, just from our adding a single 1! What gives?

The Element of Surprise

Let's think about what just happened in a slightly different way.

Imagine you were playing a game with a friend: your friend picks a number between 1 and 10, and you try to guess what it is. If your friend picked the number "8" 70 times in a row, what would you guess on the 71st time? 8, right? And you wouldn't be very surprised if 8 turned out to be the right number. But if, after 70 "8s," your friend suddenly picked a 1, you **would** be a little surprised. Right?

Well, normal compression algorithms work kind of like you guessing numbers that your friend picks. Remember that normal compression algorithms work by finding **patterns** in the data–and surprises **break patterns**, which means our normal compression algorithm has to work harder.

Our normal compression algorithm isn't **surprised** when it sees 8 for the 71st time in a row–so it has no problem compressing it into a nice small pattern. But it **is** surprised when it sees a 1 instead–which means it can't compress the data quite as much.

In fact, as Claude Shannon, the father of information theory, proved, the more **surprising** data is, the more **information** it contains. And the more **information** there is, the less a normal compression algorithm will be able to **compress** it!

But, as we'll see, Slices of Pi works a little differently–in fact, Slices of Pi doesn't mind little surprises at all–or even big ones!

Text Message from Laurie Partensky to Igor Partensky

remember 2 tell roy we have his hat make sure he knows i gave it 2 u this am but u forgot 2 take it not my fault :-)

Text Message from Roy Selva to Laurie Partensky

Hi Laurie it's Roy! Igor gave me your number. I'll be over in your area later this afternoon, I can come pick up my hat if you'll be around?

From Police Report MA2911034 (Michael Hathaway, Reporting Officer)

Mr. Igor Partensky answered the door. He appeared agitated but gave Officer Harkens and myself permission to enter and was polite and co-operative.

I told Mr. Partensky that we had received reports of a disturbance at this address. Mr. Partensky said that he had come home to pick up a contract he had forgotten that morning, and had found his boss, Mr. Roy Selva, in his bedroom. According to Mr. Partensky, Mr. Selva had only been wearing a hat.

Mr. Partensky told us he had "blown his cap" upon discovering Mr. Selva, and that Mr. Partensky's wife, Mrs. Laurie Partensky, had heard the shouting and come out of the master bathroom in her robe, which agitated Mr. Partensky further. Mrs. Partensky and Mr. Selva then locked themselves in the master bathroom to get away from Mr. Partensky.

Officer Harkens took Mr. Partensky out on the front lawn while I went upstairs to get Mrs. Partensky and Mr. Selva out of the master bathroom.

[…]

According to Mr. Selva, Mr. Partensky threatened to take the contract and "shove it up [Mr. Selva's] ass." Mr. Partensky then attempted to carry out this threat.

Medics on the scene treated Mr. Selva for minor lacerations.

Handwritten Notes of George Baniff, Attorney at Law

Igor Partensky initial meeting

(Referral from Linda White in family law–she thinks he might have a counter-case–had not even retained counsel!)

Doesn't seem to understand I practice IP, cannot keep his wife from divorcing him

"That bastard" = Ray/Roy? Selva

(Ex) Wife is Laurie

"Slices of Pie"

"Just a toy"

"Just a toy" again (so why is MMC coming after him?)

Extremely theoretical

Extremely naive

Lost copy of new contract (discovery?)

Doesn't care about $

Doesn't care about status as inventor

"I can screw bastard who screwed Laurie?"

THIS MOTIVATES

Furious, crying jags, technical mumbo jumbo mixed in

All over the road

Cannot take the stand under any circumstances

From *Slices of Pi for Total Morons*

Slices of Pi doesn't mind surprises because it doesn't work by looking for **patterns** in data like other compression algorithms. So how **does** it work?

The answer is simple: it looks for a **copy** of the data in the **digits of pi**.

Blast from the Past

You remember high school geometry class, right? Circles? Pi? All that jazz? Well, just in case you haven't even balanced your checkbook since high school, here's a quick refresher:

- Pi is the **ratio** between a circle's **diameter** (how big it is across) and its **circumference** (how big it is around)

- The value of pi is 3.14159265358 ... etc. etc. etc.

- We have to use all those etc.'s because pi is an **irrational** number, which means that the digits of pi go on **forever** ... and they **never fall into a pattern**!

Seek and You Shall Find ... in Pi!

OK, let's try out the Slices of Pi algorithm ourselves.

Say we've got some data we want to compress. For example, if we had a big ugly number like this:

6939937510582097

... then the Slices of Pi algorithm would **search** for our data in the digits of pi ...

3.14159265358979323846264338327950288419716939937510582097 49445 ...

There it is!

Once it's found our data in the digits of pi, the Slices of Pi algorithm can calculate just **two numbers** ...

- The **number of digits** of pi it had to look through before it found the start of the data (40 in this case–count it yourself, but don't forget to skip the 3 and the decimal point!)

- **How many** digits of data to read from that starting point (16–because that's how long our original data was!)

... and **compress** our big ugly number down to something much smaller and simpler:

40 16

Wow! That's a lot shorter than 6939937510582097!

Where Oh Where Has My Little Data Gone?

But woah, wait! Instead of our big ugly number, now all we've got are these two smaller numbers, 40 and 16. Where did our original data go?

Don't worry! These two numbers contain all the information that Slices of Pi needs to get us our original data back, safe and sound.

This is called **decompression**, and Slices of Pi does it by just taking the first number (40) and **skipping** that many digits in pi. Then it **reads** as many digits as the second number tells it (16) ... and voila! We get back our big ugly number, just like we started with:

6939937510582097

Thanks, Slices of Pi!

But How Does Slices of Pi Calculate All Those Digits of Pi?

Great question!

It wasn't always easy to calculate digits of pi. In fact, for most of human history, the Slices of Pi algorithm wouldn't have worked very well–it would have taken too long just to calculate the digits of pi and search through them for the data we wanted to compress.

But the advent of **quantum computing** allowed scientists and mathematicians (like Igor Partensky, the inventor of Slices of Pi!) to find tricky ways to do these calculations and searches much more quickly. **Quantum computing** is what lets Slices of Pi work so well!

(Fun fact: For a long time, people competed to calculate more and more digits of pi. Before quantum computing, the record was set in 2010 by Shigeru Kondo and Alexander J. Yee, who calculated pi to **5 trillion digits**!)

(Fun fact: Some scientists believe that quantum computing allows them to solve certain problems so quickly because it's actually spreading out all that work over **multiple parallel universes**. Talk about your collaborative efforts! Pick up a copy of *Quantum Computing for Total Morons* to learn more!)

Recap: Slices of Pi at Work

Phew, we've covered a lot of ground here! Let's take a moment to recap what we've learned.

- Unlike **normal** compression algorithms, which compress by finding **patterns** in the data, Slices of Pi works by finding a **copy** of the data in the **digits of pi**.

- **Quantum computing** is the technology that allows Slices of Pi to calculate and search through the digits of pi so quickly.

- Slices of Pi **compresses** data by turning big ugly numbers into two smaller numbers: the digit of pi where it should **start reading** to find our data, and **how many** digits to read.

Well, that wasn't so hard, was it? Slices of Pi turned out to be pretty simple! But wait: there's a twist (well what did you expect–there's **always** a twist!).

Here's a hint: what happens if we think **smaller**?

Memo from Ulysses J. Fleetwell to Stanley Reiner (CEO, Mariposa Media Conglomerate)

While I understand and appreciate your desire to pursue intellectual ownership and a subsequent patent, it is my duty to counsel you towards the legal argument that is most likely to succeed. In this case, that argument is quite clearly *not* for intellectual ownership of "Slices of Pi," but rather the pursuit of "shop right" for the algorithm.

My reasoning is as follows:

- At the time he invented the "Slices of Pi" algorithm, Mr. Partensky was employed by Mariposa Media Conglomerate as a Field Technician, Class III. Given the standard duties of a Field Technician, Class III, the court is nearly certain to refuse to classify him as an "inventive employee."

- Therefore, Mr. Partensky's inventions during his employment at Mariposa Media Conglomerate cannot generally be considered works for hire or the intellectual property of Mariposa Media Conglomerate.

- Mr. Partensky admits, however, to doing substantial development towards the "Slices of Pi" algorithm on his Toshiba Q100 laptop, for which he requested reimbursement from Mariposa Media Conglomerate–a request which Mariposa Media Conglomerate granted.

- Mr. Partensky's submission for reimbursement suggests that he viewed the laptop as primarily intended for use in the performance of his duties at Mariposa Media Conglomerate.

- In which case, Mr. Partensky invented the "Slices of Pi" algorithm largely on Mariposa Media Conglomerate's equipment and at its expense.

- In which case, the requirements for "shop right" are neatly met, and Mariposa Media Conglomerate can claim an implied license, perpetual and irrevocable, to the "Slices of Pi" algorithm.

It is true that "shop right" will not allow Mariposa Media Conglomerate to patent the "Slices of Pi" algorithm, and that this approach leaves the door open for Mariposa Media Conglomerate's competitors to employ the algorithm as well (perhaps pending separate licensing agreements with Mr. Partensky, if he chooses to pursue a patent himself).

[…]

Another consideration, and one which we should not take lightly, is the sympathetic human element. Even a seasoned intellectual property judge is unlikely to be totally immune to Mr. Partensky's appeal as the genius underdog, and Mr. Partensky's counsel, Mr. Baniff, is a deep old file with whom I have done battle before and for whom I have developed a healthy respect. He will not hesitate to exploit the human angle, and will do an excellent job of suggesting that Mariposa Media Conglomerate, by hastily offering Mr. Partensky a promotion contingent on his renouncing all interest in the "Slices of Pi" algorithm, was attempting to perform upon Mr. Partensky's person the same act which Mr. Selva later performed upon Mrs. Partensky's.

[...]

If you absolutely insist on pursuing intellectual ownership of the algorithm, rather than "shop right," we will of course craft the strongest case we can for ownership. We may be able to make the case that "Slices of Pi" is the intellectual property of Mariposa Media Conglomerate by building on the argument that Mr. Partensky developed the "Slices of Pi" algorithm at Mr. Selva's suggestion, in the hopes of producing work of sufficient value to Mariposa Media Conglomerate to justify financial compensation in the amount of the price of a laptop that he had purchased for personal use. In that case, Mr. Partensky might be viewed as a de facto "inventive employee" working under an implied contract, and the "Slices of Pi" algorithm might be viewed as a "work for hire" and therefore the sole intellectual property of Mariposa Media Conglomerate.

Do consider seriously, however, that any such case will be inherently and markedly inferior to the case for "shop right," and a riskier proposition.

In other words it may be advisable, in this case, to think smaller.

Please advise me regarding your decision at your earliest convenience.

How are Martha and the little ones? We hope to see you all in the Hamptons before Summer bids adieu and Fall comes knocking.

From *My 12 Memorable Cases (A Memoir)*, by Ulysses J. Fleetwell (unpublished)

Despite my counsel, Mr. Reiner and the other decision makers at Mariposa had chosen to swing for the fences–to make the case not for "shop right" but for intellectual ownership of "Slices of Pi." They had determined, as was their charge and no one else's, that the financial difference between these two outcomes outweighed the increased risk of the second.

My duty had been to counsel them towards caution, but once they had considered and rejected such counsel, my duty was to deliver them the verdict they had deemed necessary, by any means within my power–and this was the task to which I set myself.

[...]

In following my account of Mariposa Media Conglomerate v. Partensky thus far, gentle reader, you may have found it surprising how many legally irrelevant trivia I sought to know about Igor Partensky–his habits, his foibles, which shows he watched on which nights while dining on which foods–as it may surprise you to know that I came to like him very much.

In fact this was one of my trade secrets–which, being retired, I can now reveal: in a legal contest, it is easier to defeat an adversary for whom you feel affection. The tension that inevitably develops between that tender human feeling and your legal obligations can be put to excellent use. As an attorney it is one's legal obligation to "zealously" represent the interests of one's client, and the sharp regret at working against the interests of someone for whom one bears affection is the clearest indication I know that one is actually representing one's client with a single-mindedness and vigor that could be legitimately termed "zeal."

From *Slices of Pi for Total Morons*

A Small Twist

Let's try to compress some different data with Slices of Pi. This time we'll try to compress:

27609

That's a shorter number, so it should be pretty easy, right?

As usual, Slices of Pi starts by searching through the digits of pi for our data. This time we have to go a little further into pi–you might not want to try this at home!

... 9940012601642 **27609** 2608234930 ...

There it is! Our data starts right at digit 34211 and runs for 5 digits, so Slices of Pi will compress it to:

34211 5

No problem, we've got this! But wait ... do you notice something strange here? Let's look at the two versions of our data–original and compressed–right next to each other, this time with the spaces squeezed out:

27609
342115

You see that? The **compressed** version is actually **bigger** than our **original data**! Not exactly what we were looking for in a **compression** algorithm!

So, umm ... what's up with that, Slices of Pi?

Getting Real

In the real world, this example wouldn't cause us too much trouble–after all, "27609" is so small already–who cares if we can't compress it?

But the same kind of problem crops up when we apply Slices of Pi to all sorts of real world data: sometimes Slices of Pi has to look **so deep** into pi to find a copy of our data that the number telling us which digit our data starts at is actually **bigger** than our original data was! What can we do in that case? Well, as you might have guessed, Slices of Pi has a few more tricks up its sleeve.

Divide and Conquer

One trick that Slices of Pi can use is just to split your data up into chunks and compress each of those.

Sometimes this works, and sometimes it doesn't. But even when it doesn't, Slices of Pi still isn't ready to throw in the towel ...

Recurses, Foiled Again! (And Again, and Again, and Again ...)

The most important trick that Slices of Pi uses to solve this problem is called **recursion**. Don't be scared:

recursion is just a fancy word for an **algorithm** that can **use itself** as one of its steps.

With that in mind, let's look at that pesky original data again . . .

27609

. . . and remember that Slices of Pi "compressed" it to

34211 5

. . . which was bigger than 27609.

But what if we try **recursing**? That is, what if we take part of the **compressed** version of our data–34211–and try to compress **that** with Slices of Pi?

You know the drill by now–first Slices of Pi tries to find 34211 in the digits of pi . . . and this time, it doesn't have to look so far!

. . . 28034825 **34211** 7067 . . .

Slices of Pi finds our new data–34211–only **90 digits** into pi. It's 5 digits long, so the compressed version would be:

90 5

Hmmm . . . that's looking pretty small–definitely smaller than 34211. So what if we took the compressed version of our original data, 27609, which looked like this:

34211 5

111

... and **substituted in** our compressed version of 34211? It would look something like:

90 5 5

Let's squeeze the spaces out and compare it to our original again:

27609
9055

Hey! We've managed to make the **compressed** version smaller than the **original** version again!

Things looked dark for a moment there, but we've snatched victory from the jaws of defeat. Nice save, Slices of Pi!

From *My 12 Memorable Cases (A Memoir)*, by Ulysses J. Fleetwell (unpublished)

When an intellectual property litigator walks into a court room, he is Ishmael of the Bible, entering a state of war with all present–not just the opposing counsel and the jury, when there is one, but even his own client, with his white lies and omissions and emotions muddying every matter.

But there is one opponent against whom the attorney always enjoys an advantage, if he is clever enough to exploit it: the judge.

Yes, his honor, the sternest of the stern, the fairest of the fair, ostensibly the least interested of all those present, harbors a hidden desire–and a hidden desire, if you discover it, is a handle by which you may turn a man any way you wish.

Once upon a time his honor was like you. He earned his daily bread and the respect of his fellows through the exercise of his intellect in the legal arena, and now, as a reward for his brilliance, he has won a post where that very intellect must remain subjugated and silent. Hence why judges so love to write opinions, and will jump on any opportunity to do so–and why, when they cannot write opinions, they write books. Every minute that his honor sits on the bench, impassive and silent, his intellect grows increasingly anxious and longs for exercise. It will not be denied forever.

[...]

So while it is nearly impossible to manipulate a judge by means of what you *say*–his raw intellect is at least a match for yours, and paces his skull like a caged panther, desperate for any chance to escape and tear your feeble reasoning to shreds–you may often manipulate even an excellent and impartial judge by the judicious exercise of *what you leave out*.

[...]

In my closing argument to Mariposa Media Conglomerate v. Partensky, I flirted with an idea, approaching it from several angles but never quite arriving at it. It was an idea without any legal weight whatsoever–an idea whose only merit was a certain wit, a certain turning of the themes of the case back upon the case itself. Had I employed this idea in my closing argument, Judge Bulger would have discounted it, immediately and appropriately. But dangling there–unstated, unconsummated–the idea was a lure, an irresistible promise of exercise for his honor's restless intellect.

From the Decision of Mariposa Media Conglomerate v. Partensky (by the Honorable Marcus Whitney Bulger)

In closing, I must note the irony of Mr. Partensky's counter-claims in light of the fact that the very method he invented and purports to own–the "Slices of Pi" compression algorithm–depends upon the pre-existence of all conceivable data–whether those data describe a movie, a song, or even an invention–in the digits of pi. We presume, for example, that the "Slices of Pi" compression algorithm must *itself* be found encoded somewhere in that endless march of numbers–and that furthermore it has always been there, waiting for us to *discover*, not *invent* it. In this light the very concept of "invention" is meaningless outside the legal sphere–and inside the legal sphere, the concept of "invention" is neither more nor less than an exercise in the application of certain contractual laws and the rights and responsibilities they confer. In this case those laws, while subtle, are clear.

From *Slices of Pi for Total Morons*

Dealing with Loss

In the real world, loss is always a sad thing–but when it comes to compression algorithms, loss can actually be a great tool to help us make our data **even smaller**!

How does that work?

Compression algorithms come in two flavors: **lossless** and **lossy**. Slices of Pi is a **lossy** compression algorithm, which means that when you compress data with Slices of Pi, the data you get back after decompression might be **just a little different** than the data you started with. In other words, a little bit of your original data might have been **lost**.

But wait, why would you ever **choose** to lose data? Simple! Because lossy compression algorithms can often make your data **even smaller** than lossless compression algorithms–and after all, making your data small is the whole point of compression!

Sure, for some kinds of data you never want to lose anything, and then you would use a **lossless** algorithm. But for other kinds of data–like photos, videos, and music–you won't even notice a little loss. You'll sure notice the extra space on your hard drive and the quicker downloads, though!

Getting Lossy–the Normal Compression Way

You remember that normal compression algorithms work by finding **patterns** in data, and that broken patterns–or **surprises**–are harder for them to compress.

So some normal compression algorithms are **lossy** because they **smooth out** little wrinkles and surprises in the data to make more **patterns**. For example, a normal compression algorithm might be **lossy** by smoothing "1112111" into "1111111," which is more **patterned** and much easier to compress.

But remember–unlike normal compression algorithms, Slices of Pi doesn't work by finding patterns!

Choosing to Lose–the Slices of Pi Way

So if Slices of Pi doesn't care about patterns, why is it even **lossy** at all? Well, because sometimes Slices of Pi can find **slight variations** on your data much **earlier** in the digits of pi–and remember that the **earlier** Slices of Pi finds your data, the **smaller** it can make it!

(By the way, don't worry: Slices of Pi is careful to make sure that those slight variations don't affect the quality of your video or audio too much.)

So I guess you could say, when it comes to Slices of Pi: loss is a win!

From "Irrational Beauties: the Verse and Person of Ulysses Fleetwell"

Off camera: Did you ever actually meet him?

Nick Caverly: Yeah, I met him once. I'd been out of school for, like, three years, and *Unreasoning Songs* was like my Bible at the time, so I screwed up my courage and found his work address and emailed to ask if he would meet me for a beer. I emailed him like four times over a month without an answer, but finally his secretary emailed back with a time and place–some high-end "establishment" in the financial district. No beers on the menu, either, by the way–just cocktails. I think the cheapest was like $20, which is what I ordered–it was pink and really sweet. Pretty nasty.

He got there like 20 minutes late, and when they led him to the table he looked me up and down–I was dressed pretty much the same as I am right now–and he kind of sniffed, and I was like "How about you take a look at your own self, man? You look like you just came from a funeral." And he–I'll never forget this–just looked me right in the eyes for like 30 seconds, and then said: "I just came from a funeral."

Off camera: Was he serious?

Nick Caverly: Yeah, man, he was serious as a heart attack. So I'm tripping all over myself to apologize, and I'm like "Was it someone you knew well?" And he says "I knew him quite well: I killed him." Then he orders his drink.

Off camera: Wow.

Nick Caverly: Yeah, you're (bleep) right wow.

Off camera: But he was just messing with you, right?

Nick Caverly: I guess, but I don't know–that's all he would say about it. He just moved right on and asked me what my "motive" was for wanting to meet him–I remember, that was the word he used.

First I tried telling him I was just a big fan, etc. etc. etc., but he was having none of that–he was smart about people, you could tell that right away. He could really read them. Finally I broke down and admitted that I'd wanted to ask him to take a look at some of my poetry, and maybe write me a recommendation for Iowa–you know, only if he liked what he read, no pressure, etc.

So I gave him some poems, which he folded and stuffed in his inside pocket–presumably to toss in the first trash can he passed–and then he asked me a couple questions about who I was reading and so on, and that was that. Oh, and he paid for our drinks, so that was nice I guess.

Off Camera: Did he (inaudible)?

Nick Caverly: Did he what?

Off Camera: Did he write a recommendation for you?

Nick Caverly (laughing): Naw, man, he never wrote anything for me. I mean, except the poems. Those he wrote for all of us, right?

From *Posthumous and Uncollected Poems of Ulysses Fleetwell*

Forgiveness, like light,
Has a speed:
If we flee our sins too quickly it cannot
Overtake us

[…]

Hurtling away from all things
At the speed of forgiveness
Plus one
I can see him still–
Gigantic and ursine
Even slouched in defeat,
Wild eyes searching for an ally
As a dancing bear
Might search the audience
For one look of compassion
Before the whip
Cracked

[…]

But the numbers go forever
Counting all things done
And all things undone
In their endless flow of
Everywhere and everywhen:
All things as they are and were,
All things as they should have been

Note, in its Entirety, Found on Igor Partensky's Kitchen Counter

My dearest Ida,

From Wikipedia's "Igor Partensky" Page

This article has multiple issues. Please help improve it or discuss these issues on the talk page.
[…]

Death

[…]
After his legal defeat and divorce, Partensky withdrew from public view. His behavior became increasingly erratic[according to whom?].
[…]
Police estimated that the car was traveling at over 70 MPH when it struck the tree. Vodka was found in the car, and Partensky's blood alcohol level was measured at 0.4, over 4 times the legal limit in Massachusetts.

Legacy

Partensky's daughter, Ida, studied intellectual property law at Georgetown University. Inspired by her father's misfortune[source?], she established the "Igor Partensky Project for Intellectual Honesty," a non-profit entity that represents individual inventors *pro bono* and lobbies for intellectual property reform.

The Project[split to new page?] has achieved several notable and much-needed reforms[biased or partisan attitude?] and is currently[clarify time frame] engaged in an ongoing class-action suit against Mariposa Media Conglomerate.

In order to maintain impartiality, the Project does not accept outside funding, and operates solely off their large original donation[source?].

The original donor has chosen to remain anonymous.

Future Perfect

The cookies had been baked in the shape of butterflies, but then frosted with asymmetric black and white designs and piled carelessly on a pewter tray as if to conceal the resemblance. Butterflies had been stitched in stout black thread on the headpieces of the black leather chairs distributed around the oval conference table, from whose wavy wooden grain distorted butterflies seemed desperate to escape. The trash can opened by means of a rotating panel attached with screws at what would have been the head and tip of the abdomen. A beam of sun at just the right angle released an engraved horde from the frosted glass above the door, and even the carpet, Janine Smalls noticed, sported a suspiciously papilionaceous weave. She was squinting at the ceiling, searching for butterflies in the plaster, when someone opened the door so violently that the breeze compelled her to close her eyes.

"Miss Smalls, Mr. Bradley," said the small round man who rode in on the breeze, "please don't get up! Jerome Pope, CEO, so sorry to have kept you waiting, but how excellent to put faces to names! And such faces! When we spoke on the phone"–this to Janine

Smalls–"I had no idea I was talking to a displaced movie star. And Mr. Bradley, before today we have exchanged only emails, but I imagined you *just* as you are–the corn-fed Midwestern boy made good, all warmth and casual charm. So," he said as he took a seat across the table, "how many did you count?"

Almost without moving her head Janine Smalls glanced at Ryan Bradley, in case he wanted to field the question, but at the slight suggestion of furrow in his brow she jumped in.

"How many emails?" she asked.

"Butterflies, Miss Smalls!" said Mr. Pope, sounding somehow like a movie Nazi. "How many butterflies. Some of our clients have counted hundreds."

"We're not clients," Mr. Bradley said.

"Not yet. But you can still count the butterflies if you'd like. That's free."

Mr. Bradley shifted in his seat, as if seeking a fortified position from which to attack, and Miss Smalls spoke before he could settle.

"Mr. Pope, why don't we get right to it and take a look at the campaign?"

"Before you do," said Mr. Bradley, "it might be good to do a little level-setting. If I were in your position, I'd want to know right off the bat where I stood, so I'm going to be honest with you: I'm only here because of the tremendous respect I have for Janine. She–cover your ears, Janine–is the one who brought the Upkeeper back from the brink–no, Janine, I don't mind saying it–with her 'Man the Towers' campaign. So if she tells me you've got a way for us to finally win the hearts and minds of that elusive 18 to 25 year old crowd, then fine, I'll take a look at it.

If she asks me to fly half way across the country to see this mysterious campaign, instead of you coming to present it to us–perverting the natural order of things–all right, I do it. That's how much respect I have for her. But at heart I'm still an old-school, facts-and-figures type CEO–I believe in sales and smart spends with measurable ROI. I get a little nervous around all this pie-in-the-sky touchy-feely branding talk, and even my tremendous respect for Janine only buys you so much: one pitch, to be exact. And it better be quick, and it had better be killer, because as far as I'm concerned you're starting out with two strikes against you."

"If I'm pitching," said Mr. Pope, "wouldn't that be three balls against me?"

"I beg your pardon?"

"Your honesty is refreshing, Mr. Bradley, and I appreciate it, as I appreciate the limits of your schedule and attention. And luckily here is Dr. Novak joining us, just in time. Dr. Novak, do you have the envelope?"

Dr. Novak had just burst through the door at something approximating a sprint–a speed he managed with a grace unusual for a pasty 40 year old in a lab coat, until he caught sight of Janine Smalls tossing her hair, at which point he slammed into the conference table.

"I'm sorry," said Dr. Novak, to the table first, then to the assembly, except Miss Smalls, whose eyes he had trouble meeting, "I'm sorry. The printer was, uh, low on the tungsten ink."

He handed a manila envelope to Mr. Pope and sat down next to him, springing up once briefly to close the door he had left open and mismanaging the chair upon his return.

"Our Dr. Novak may lack grace navigating furniture," Mr. Pope said, "but I assure you that on the mental plane he is a Baryshnikov."

"Is that guy ... " Mr. Bradley caught himself and turned from Miss Smalls to address Dr. Novak directly. "Are you a marketer in a lab coat?"

"Dr. Novak is a scientist," said Mr. Pope. "Our chief scientist, in fact, and his research is what makes everything we do here at Future Perfect Branding possible. We are more than just marketers here, Mr. Bradley–the science is what makes us different. And now," he continued, unwrapping a string that had been wound three times around the cardboard clasp of the manila envelope, "perhaps you'd like to leave the matter of Dr. Novak's fashion behind and take a look at what I like to call the 'future perfect' of the Upkeeper brand."

He slid a single sheet of paper across the conference table, and, at Miss Smalls's urging, Mr. Bradley picked it up.

"It looks like some kind of page from a comic book," he said.

"It *is* a page from a comic book. Or rather, it will be. Or rather," said Mr. Pope with a significant look at Dr. Novak, "it *will have been*."

"You've lost me," Mr. Bradley said.

"Don't put it down–look more carefully. Do you recognize the superheroine in the center panel? The one standing akimbo and triumphant over the heap of crumpled villains?"

"Looks like, what's her name ... Stupenda."

126

"Very good, Mr. Bradley. What you are holding in your hand is Stupenda's first appearance, in fact, in the now extremely valuable Thrilling Tales #24, before the public's response made the editors conclude that she merited her own title. But do you notice anything different about her?"

Mr. Bradley peered at the page for a moment, squinting and muttering, and handed it to Miss Smalls.

"Janine, comics aren't really my thing. You see what he's getting at?"

"They've adjusted her costume to look like the Upkeeper," she said.

"Exactly!" Mr. Pope struck the air with his finger as if ringing a bell. "The subtle crenelations along the top of her breast line, you see them? The uptick along the bottom into the breastbone. Exactly as if she were wearing an Upkeeper bra." He sat back and folded his small red hands on his belly, as if to say "And there you have it."

There was silence in the conference room for a moment, during which Mr. Bradley sought Miss Smalls's eyes, which were otherwise occupied drilling holes in Mr. Pope.

"But explain to him about . . . " said Miss Smalls.

"I have to tell you," broke in Mr. Bradley, looking at Mr. Pope but speaking as if to Miss Smalls, "I'm underwhelmed on a couple fronts here. I don't see how co-opting Stupenda is going to get us the 18 to 25 year olds–and that's even if we could afford the licensing, which is, heh, out of the question. But beyond that, for us to fly all the way out here and be presented with a single page of comic book art, that's–I mean, it's not even finished comic book art. There's no color, the speech balloons aren't even filled in ... "

"Ah, Mr. Bradley," said Mr. Pope, "in fact this page is very much finished, and at considerable expense. These might appear like ordinary ink and paper to you, but they are not–both are our own proprietary formula, infused with tungsten and other rare earth elements ... "

Dr. Novak pursed his lips.

"... to help them survive the rigors of their journey."

"Journey? What are you going to do with them?" said Mr. Bradley. "Throw them from moving vans? Crop dust cities?"

"Think bigger."

"I know, you're going to put them on the moon. That would be just about perfect. How on Earth did you get mixed up with these people, Janine?"

"Have you ever read Ray Bradbury's classic story 'A Sound of Thunder?'" asked Mr. Pope. "It's something of a seminal text for us here at Future Perfect Brands. In fact, we take our logo–the butterfly–from that very story. Imagine: a hunter traveling back through time with the goal of killing a dinosaur, the fiercest prey of all–a Tyrannosaurus Rex. But it is a very specific Tyrannosaurus Rex that he must kill–one that is already on the edge of death. If he were to kill a healthy animal, who might have lived longer without his intervention, the hunter runs the risk of disturbing the course of history, with who knows what paradoxical results back in the present. All goes to plan until suddenly, in his haste, the hunter steps off his carefully laid path and crushes a Jurassic butterfly.

But it's just a butterfly–just a single, tiny butterfly–how much could its death matter? Quite a bit, as the hunter discovers upon returning to the present. The effect of that one butterfly's death, seemingly so trivial, has cascaded and amplified through time–altering the course of history and changing entirely the world he used to know."

"I'm not following you ... "

"We send the paper into the past," said Dr. Novak. "That's the journey that Mr. Pope means. So far we've only managed to send paper and ink reliably, and only after treating it to withstand what we call 'temporal dis ...' "

"To a very particular point in the past," said Mr. Pope, talking over him. "June 3rd, 1941, to be exact, when issue #24 of Thrilling Tales had just left the inker and was waiting on the colorist's desk. From there our subtly altered Stupenda will be decked out in her trademark fire-engine reds and school-bus yellows, and when she goes to press she will be wearing what appears to be an Upkeeper bra. As she charms her way into readers' hearts, becoming a fan favorite and commanding her own book, our altered design will go with her, as part of her iconic appearance. And like the butterfly's death in Bradbury's story, this one tiny change will ripple out, compound, and snowball–into a great swell of present demand for the Upkeeper."

Mr. Pope slapped his open palm on the table, as if announcing gin.

Mr. Bradley opened his mouth as if to speak, but nothing came out.

"Imagine," Mr. Pope continued before he could recover, "that you are a 20 year old girl walking into a clothing store. You're still humming the Lay-Z song you were listening to in your car, the one that contains the lyric 'If you diss me I'll upend yuh, I got guns like Stupenda.' You aren't thinking of Stupenda consciously, or how she has become a feminist icon, more powerful than the men she battles precisely because of the erotic femininity that her suit makes no attempt to disguise. But somewhere in the back of your mind a golden and fire-engine red archetype is billowing about, and when you see the Upkeeper hanging on the rack–those distinctive lines–a connection arcs in your brain, and you think 'Yes, yes, this is a bra that understands that there's nothing contradictory about a woman being powerful and feminine at the same time, that understands how needing a man and wanting to attract one aren't the same thing at all.' What other brand would you possibly buy?"

"Just so I'm sure I've got this," said Mr. Bradley, "you're telling me that you'll send that piece of paper back in time and change the past, and then all of a sudden, magically, hordes of 18 to 25 year old women will be buying the Upkeeper here, now–today. Is there a hidden camera in here? Am I on television?"

"No," said Dr. Novak, despite Mr. Pope's ostentatious waving off, "that's not how it works. We can't change the past of this world-line. It's already happened. When we send something back, a whole new world-line splits off–a new universe. Like–like a new fork in a river. We won't experience it, but it *will* exist. So if we send this page back, everything that Mr. Pope described will happen in a parallel world–or more precisely what we call an alternate retrograde timeline. Alternate, because it's not ours, and retrograde, because ... "

"You mean," said Mr. Bradley, "that after all the hogwash and sci-fi snake oil, you're not even *pretending* to offer me sales?"

"You'll have sales, just not in this world-line."

"Sales in another dimension? ROI in the Twilight Zone? I got to hand it to you gentlemen, I have heard some pitches in my day, but this takes the cake. Fellas, thank you for your time, this conversation is over. I'm going to catch the early flight."

As he stood up, Miss Smalls put her hand on his forearm, and at her touch Mr. Bradley jumped and twisted as if her fingers coursed with fire. She took the hand away and ran it through her hair, as if putting the entire situation into some semblance of arrangement, and Mr. Bradley fell back into his chair, flustered.

"Just hear him out, Ryan" said Miss Smalls to Mr. Bradley, "for my sake. Give him two more minutes."

Mr. Bradley, his cheeks still red and eyes still squarely on his shoes, nodded, and Mr. Pope, sensing profit in confusion, sprang from his chair like a musician about to solo.

"What are the truly great discoveries of the modern age?" he asked the room. "The low-hanging fruit of science has been picked. Today's scientists are grinders, mining nature's secrets by the sweat of their brow instead of the dynamite of their intellect, and the discoveries they do manage–present company excluded of course, Dr. Novak–are decidedly stones of the semi-precious variety.

"The plastic arts? Never has 'plastic' been an apter term. Throw a can of paint at a canvas or urinate on an Alsatian husky, and you too can be a plastic artist.

"Meanwhile those who work in literature and film seem to be the only ones on the planet who practice recycling with deadly seriousness.

"And as for music, may I remind you that not five minutes ago I quoted from a popular artist of the day who saw fit to rhyme 'upend yuh' with 'Stupenda.' "

"He also rhymed it with 'unfriend yuh' in the same song," said Dr. Novak.

"In the *same song*," said Mr. Pope, shaking his head. "But despite all our crimes and mediocrities, I believe that future ages will look back on us kindly for one reason and one reason only–because it was in our lifetimes that humankind discovered the Brand."

Mr. Pope paused to gauge Mr. Bradley's reaction, but it seemed that he was still recovering from the touch of Janine Smalls.

"And it was a discovery, not an invention," Mr. Pope continued. "It has been there for some time now, the next step in evolution, quietly waiting for us to notice it, as we might have waited for the apes to notice us. It waited as we fumbled about, speaking of a 'brand of this' or a 'brand of that,' as one might talk about 'freedom to speak' or 'love of horses'–without realizing that one is missing the big idea. Freedom with a capital F. Love with a capital L. Brand," here he paused, as if inviting any member of the audience to fill in for him, "with a capital B.

"And that is what we're offering you today. The instant we send this page back in time, a *whole other universe* comes into being, one which owes its *entire in-*

ception to the Upkeeper Brand. And as we continue to work together, finding creative and unique branding opportunities like Stupenda, this universe is just the first of many–a whole constellation of universes built on the Upkeeper brand.

"Any CEO can track sales and ROI, but today I invite you to think bigger than that. Can you believe in the Upkeeper brand–can you believe that it is a Brand with a capital 'B'–something bigger than a single world, a force that spans and spawns whole universes? Or would you rather take the early flight, return home, take out a half page ad in the latest teen magazine–even a full page, perhaps!–scraping and scrapping to move a few more units in Target and Wal-Mart this quarter? The choice is yours."

For a second it appeared that Mr. Pope was going to add something, but then–perhaps in response to the subtle shake of Miss Smalls's head–he stopped.

"I rest my case," he said, and sat down.

"Janine," said Mr. Bradley, who had managed to look up from his shoes somewhere around *love with a capital L,* "did you know this was the pitch before we came out here?"

Now it was her gaze that fell.

"I expected better from you, Janine."

"Can we talk about this?" she said.

"What's there to talk about? You had us fly out here on our own dime, when you knew *this* was what they were putting on the table?"

"Should we step out and give them a moment?" Dr. Novak asked Mr. Pope. The latter shook his head and put a finger to his lips.

"Ryan, you don't understand," said Miss Smalls.

"You're damn right I don't understand."

"I know how much this company means to you."

"I don't think you do know–my brother and I built this whole business from the ground up, and yes, we've hit some tough times, I'm the first to admit that–but I am at a loss for how ... "

"I understand that, and I understand how you think you're honoring your brother's memory, but you're not going to survive in this market without adaptation–real, *fundamental* change–and you won't change *anything*. The name? No, we can't change that, Jack came up with it. The design? No, we can't change that, that was Jack's, it's perfect as it is. How about a new model? No, Jack envisioned the Upkeeper as the only bra you'll ever need–we can't reconcile that message with an expanded line. I want to help you save the Upkeeper–I really do–but I can't if you take away all my options."

"The models that Jack designed were perfect when he designed them, and they're perfect now. Women's breasts haven't changed. He was the designer, you're the marketer. Your job is not to change the design–it's to make the world understand that the design is perfect."

"You see what I mean?" It seemed she was appealing to Mr. Pope and Dr. Novak as much as to Mr. Bradley now. "You think about this business with your heart, not your head, and because of that the Upkeeper isn't going to exist at all in a year or two. So when Mr. Pope pitched me I thought, yes, it sounded crazy–but frankly, not too much crazier than changing nothing and just expecting the world to adapt to *us*. I thought that maybe–just maybe–you would see this as a way to let the Upkeeper survive, unchanged, exactly as Jack envisioned it. Not here–but somewhere. And I hoped that, since your head wasn't really involved too much in running the business these days, this might be enough for–for your heart."

Mr. Bradley stood up and buttoned his sports coat.

"Gentlemen," he said, "best of luck to you–you'll need it. Janine, it seems we no longer have anything to offer you at Upkeeper Inc. I'll arrange your last paycheck and any other details when I get back. Now please excuse me."

"Why are the machines running?" asked Mr. Pope.

Dr. Novak, still drying his hands, started and nearly hit his head on the low doorway of the lab's once-closet-now-restroom.

"What do you want? We agreed that the lab is off limits to you."

"Yes, our famous 'agreement.' In fact, I was just stopping by on my way out to remind you, precisely, about our agreement–about how we had *agreed* that you would leave the sales to me, and that, when you were invited into the sales room, you were there for very specific purposes: to wear your lab coat and stutter charmingly, to lend an air of scientific respectability to the proceedings, and to answer any specific technical questions that might come up, about–for example–the manufacture of the tungsten ink and paper, or the other rare earth elements. But now I find myself with a more pressing question: why are the machines running? What are you sending back?"

"It's nothing. Something for a client."

"We don't have any clients."

"I was just trying to help, you know," said Dr. Novak. "Mr. Bradley seemed confused and insulted, so I thought I would explain."

"Of course he was confused and insulted–he was meant to be. I was combining two powerful and counterintuitive sales techniques: the vision play and the negative sell. You are not expected to understand this. You are expected to play your role. When you don't, you cost us sales–like today's. Now, stop changing the subject: why are the machines running?"

Dr. Novak checked a gauge and sighed.

"I thought that if he'd read it, things might have gone differently today."

"If *who* had read *what*?"

"If Mr. Bradley had read 'A Sound of Thunder'–then he might have understood what we do. So I printed up a tungsten copy of the June 1952 issue of *Collier's* and I'm sending it back to his room, when he's twelve. He'll read the story, grow up with it in the back of his mind, and then maybe your pitch will make more sense to him."

"How can you possibly justify this insane waste of resources?"

"We might get a new customer out of it."

"In another world," said Mr. Pope.

"Of course–in an alternate retrograde world-line. Just like we offer our clients."

"Dr. Novak, I could not care less whether a different Mr. Bradley purchases services from a different me–and I *know* that you could not care less, either: you have maligned our value proposition too many times in my hearing. Why are you really sending the magazine back?"

Dr. Novak took off his glasses and cleaned the lenses on his lab coat.

"Dr. Novak?"

"All right, fine: I thought it might help Miss Smalls–in an alternate retrograde world-line, but still. She championed us, and lost her job because of it, and I just thought–it would be a nice thing to do for her."

Mr. Pope narrowed his eyes and steeled his gaze.

"This run will come out of your paycheck," he said. "Future Perfect Brands is not going to foot the bill for some schoolboy crush you've developed."

"What paycheck? We haven't paid ourselves for three months."

"Your equity, then."

"Fine with me," said Dr. Novak. "You want it all? What's 50 percent of 0?"

"I have a meeting with some potential investors," said Mr. Pope. "They are only in from Moscow for one night, and I prefer not to arrive upset and frustrated when so much is on the line. We'll discuss this further in the morning."

"I don't think we will," said Dr. Novak, coming closer. "I don't think we'll discuss it tomorrow, or the day after, or ever again. I'm done. You can tell these potential investors of yours that besides an infusion of cash, you need a new chief scientist."

"Dr. Novak, I think perhaps you need to calm ... "

"I don't need to do anything except get away from here–and from you. How did I even let you talk me into this venture? It's insane–a perversion of my work."

"*Let* me talk you into this venture? When I found you, you were nothing but an underfunded, dead-end researcher in a second-rate university! I gave you the means to make your research real. I gave you an opportunity to commercialize your ideas. And this is how you express your gratitude?"

"Get out," said Dr. Novak, pushing Mr. Pope into the hallway. "I mean it. Get out! Out!"

Mr. Pope recovered his footing and turned around.

"If you take anything," he said, "and I mean *anything*, I'll have you in court for the rest of your life."

Dr. Novak slammed the door in his face.

"Oh, and one more thing," he shouted through the door, "tungsten isn't a rare earth metal!"

"Well," Mr. Pope shouted back, "it should be!"

Dr. Novak listened as Mr. Pope's footsteps faded down the hall. He was still standing there a few minutes later, letting his breathing slow and the fire leave his cheeks, when a tinny "ding"–like that of a cheap microwave–marked the finish of the run. The lights in the lab brightened noticeably, the surface of the coffee he had left on the lab bench calmed and unwrinkled, and the dull whine of the machines faded and finally stopped altogether.

In the silence that followed, Dr. Novak felt the stirrings of an old anxiety–the same anxiety that had sidled up to him in the moment he had received each of his three diplomas. He felt as if he were standing on deck looking out over an open sea–that same endless, open glare that had inspired his twelve year old self to forswear any future fishing trips. What would he do tomorrow, if he didn't come here to the lab as usual?

What about the day after? For that matter, what would he do *tonight*, without any work to bring home?

Beset by such thoughts, Dr. Novak took his time rustling up a cardboard box from the storeroom. He had almost finished packing the few possessions he cared to bring with him–some notebooks, the chipped mug he had lifted from his undergraduate lab–when the attack hit. His vision blurred and doubled, a wave of nausea surged up from his stomach, and along the center line of his head he felt as if someone had delivered a sharp blow with a huge mallet and chisel. No doubt about it: this was what dying felt like, and as one scientific corner of his mind, out of habit, considered distance to various phones and the slim survival odds, the rest of his mental energy was consumed not by fear but regret: how could he have been so afraid a few moments ago, when life had once more spread out before him, pathless and infinitely possible? He fell to the ground, crying not because of the pain but the wasted years, the missed opportunities, the cowardice and smallness of it all.

And then, as suddenly as the attack had started, it was gone, leaving no aftereffects but a metallic taste in his mouth and a few beads of sweat on his brow. For a good five minutes Dr. Novak continued to lie in the same spot and attitude, at first wondering whether he were already dead, then expecting the attack to recommence. Finally, almost in embarrassment, he stood up, testing his strength slowly but finding nothing out of order.

All was–it seemed–just fine, and there was nothing else to do but finish his preparations as if nothing out of the ordinary had happened. Which he did, though with an aura of strangeness he could not quite shake.

He was just about to turn out the lights for the last time, pausing to look back over the lab that had been his real home these last few years, when he saw it: there at the edge of his lab bench, where nothing had been a moment ago, was a slip of paper, and on the paper–in the subtle sheen of tungsten ink and his own handwriting–Janine Smalls's name and telephone number.

Other Copenhagens

At the moment when Dr. Gibbs decided it was too late to call him, Derek Field was still very much awake, and his phone–which he had tossed on the passenger seat beside the warm six pack (now five pack) of Heineken–was switched on. But even if Dr. Gibbs had called, and even if the ring tone had managed to cut through the Phil Collins blasting from the radio, Derek would not have answered. He would not have wanted to explain to the psychiatrist treating his gambling disorder why, in direct violation of every piece of clinical advice Dr. Gibbs had ever given him, as well as all common sense, Derek was speeding westward along the Mass Pike, open container in hand, on his way to a casino.

As the car climbed a long, slow hill, Derek glanced back at the few remaining lights of the city in his rear view mirror and began to sing, snapping his head forward on the beat and belting at the top of his voice.

"I can feel it, *com*-in' in the air, fuck *you* ... *Bos*-ton ..."

Just in case Boston had not gotten the message, he wedged the can of Heineken between his thighs, rolled down his window, and gave the entire city the finger, holding it, holding it high even as his hand ached from the cold wind and then went numb, holding it until he had crested the hill and that pathetic excuse for a night skyline had dropped safely behind.

Although this level of vitriol was something recent, Derek had never had much good to say about Boston. During his first 32 years of life he had thought of the place mainly as the home of the pesky Red Sox, whose drunken fans had always insisted that some "rivalry" existed between their glorified farm club and the expensive, well-oiled win-machine known as the Yankees. In recent years, Derek had been forced to admit that the Red Sox had finally learned to spend, which softened his critique somewhat. But even during the three years since he had moved here to become Dr. Gibbs's patient, Derek had never come to feel comfortable or easy on the Beantown streets, and for the last few months he had rarely left his Commonwealth Avenue apartment except to keep his weekly sessions with Dr. Gibbs, or–when he could not face another delivered meal–to visit one of the restaurants or the specialty grocery on Newbury Street.

New York had always made sense to Derek. In New York he could never be sure that a passerby on the teeming street–no matter how bad the fabric or tight the fit of his suit, no matter how torn or dirty her jeans, no matter how closely he might resemble a junkie staggering through his last days–was not in fact an entrepreneur returning from a brunch where he had just sold his third company, or a supermodel on her way to a go-see, or a recording artist with the accumulated royalties from ten platinum records tucked away somewhere in savvy investments, earning eight percent. This state of affairs appealed to Derek. It was natural; he understood it. No other city in the history of the world had approached the sophistication of New York, because no other city enjoyed such a correct and widespread understanding of what constituted personal worth.

In New York you had an entire metropolis–eight million people plus–who argued about everything, who shouted at each other from bikes and jostled each other in the subway and stole each other's cabs at rush hour, who picked each other's pockets and wagered away each other's retirement funds–but who were, beneath this surface strife, brothers and sisters in a way that no outsider could participate in or perhaps even comprehend. Because to be a New Yorker was to understand money. It was to understand that money was so important, so essential, that it did not need to be flaunted, or even displayed–like courage, it had only to be possessed. Of course the streets of Manhattan were laid out with such order and harmony. What else would one expect from a populace so sane and well-adjusted, so strong on the fundamentals?

In Boston, on the other hand, matters were inverted and sinister. Here puritanical savages walked the switchback, provincial streets, toting–instead of secret stashes of cash–concealed brains. In Boston, Derek could never be sure that the apparently homeless man who had just burst from the alley was not actually a storied MIT professor, or that the contents of the shopping cart with which he had nearly run Derek down were not a perpetual motion solution to the world's energy crisis, the blueprints for which–and this was the transgression that Derek could least overlook–the professor would undoubtedly publish free on the Internet for the benefit of an undeserving world.

Derek did not hold it against Boston that it was a poorer city than New York, but he could not excuse that Boston did not seem embarrassed by that fact. Behind all the cultural snobbery and Brahmanism lay a simple failure to recognize that the purpose of the brain–the entire human nervous system in fact, and the squishy apparatus it animated–was to make money, and that any other use was frivolous at best, and at worst obscene.

Despite this fundamental antipathy, for three years Derek had done his best to tolerate Boston and its culture of concealed brains, because Dr. Gibbs himself was very much of Boston–in appearance more like a second-generation Dunkin' Donuts mogul than a nationally known psychiatrist with a best-selling book to his name–and Dr. Gibbs's concealed brains were Derek's last best hope to break the Curse. And in the end Derek had not been the one to shatter this uneasy peace. It was Boston who had broken the truce–Boston had made it personal.

Five days ago, experiencing a rare bout of cabin fever, Derek had decided to kill some time wandering around Copley Square before his appointment with Dr. Gibbs. The weather had been cold but bright, and the bitter wind kept everyone so bundled up that, if he didn't look too closely, Derek could almost imagine New Yorkers under the mufflers and overcoats. He had not been enjoying himself exactly, but he had, for a moment, almost relaxed. Walking a little taller, looking around for once at the passersby and the buildings instead of at his shoes, for just a moment he had let his guard down. And Boston, sensing its chance, had pounced.

Derek had never been vain about his looks or ashamed by them—in almost any room with 100 randomly chosen men he would have ranked himself 50th without pride or envy. Naturally he examined his own reflection multiple times in the course of a day for purposes of basic grooming—and occasionally he would note a new gray hair, or some extra sag beneath his eyes, and reflect for a moment that he was not growing any younger. But he had never on any of those occasions seen anything remotely like the figure that stared back at him that day from the street-level glass of the Hancock Building.

It was not that his paunch had grown—he had always been a largish man—but that there was no longer anything in his weight that spoke to unsatisfied or insatiable appetites. This was defeated weight, weight that sagged and jiggled through the motions without immediate financial purpose. It was not that his eyes appeared tired and bleary—but that they did not even widen in horror as he absorbed his own image. Those were the eyes of a man in the grandstand at Suffolk Downs, registering no reaction whatsoever as the pony on which he had put the rent drifted further and further behind the pack. Those were the eyes of a man so beaten down by life that he merely wished to become one with the pavement—a man who no longer even had the spirit to shrink from fortune's blows. In other words, what Derek saw—painted in hellish, hyper-realistic color on the blue-black glass of this Boston landmark—was the portrait of a degenerate.

A defeatist. An addict. A *gambler*. If there had been a rock to hand at that moment, Derek would have hurled it.

The vision in the Hancock glass was Derek's wake up call–his moment of clarity–his rock bottom. He had understood in that instant that there could be no more peaceful co-existence, neither with the Curse or the town colluding with it. The Curse was not satisfied having taken his job. It was not satisfied having driven him from his home, the only sane city in the world. And it would *never* be satisfied, it would never stop: not until it had taken his soul. It was the Curse or Derek–there was no third option.

In that moment a plan had dropped, full-formed, into Derek's mind, like a plop of snow from a concrete ledge–an insane, inadvisable plan with little except desperation to recommend it, but still: a plan.

Derek's first thought was to tell Dr. Gibbs all about the plan–to get the psychiatrist's take, his encouragement, perhaps his suggestions for refinement. Derek was so excited by the prospect that he could not even wait the half hour until their appointment started–he had to call Dr. Gibbs right then. But as Derek, already having dialed, waited for Dr. Gibbs to pick up, he saw how telling Dr. Gibbs anything would be impossible–because if the plan did not succeed in breaking the Curse, Derek would only have the heart for one remaining option: the dark, ultimate option that no psychiatrist could ever allow any patient to consider. Dr. Gibbs could not be involved in such an enterprise, for his own sake as much as for Derek's. So when the psychiatrist answered, Derek doctored his voice to sound as sick as he was able and–the lie sitting bitter and heavy in his stomach–reported that he was having a difference of opinion with one of last night's oysters and would have to miss their appointment that week.

That same day he had begun liquidating everything: investments, property, art. In just under 48 largely sleepless hours he had sold his apartments in Boston and New York, as they were–furniture, clothes, paintings, cookware, bedding, and all other contents included–at an insane loss, for cash. He sold the BMW for 5,000 dollars–again, in cash. The contents of his storage unit went for "best offer" on Craigslist, which turned out to be: one dollar, cash. He closed his bank accounts, dissolved the equity interest in his former employer, and sold off his baseball card collection at a struggling comic book shop for a figure that kept the owner suspended for half an hour between greed and suspicion. Cash, cash, and cash. As of today, all Derek owned were the clothes on his back, a six pack–now four pack–of Dutch beer, and the two duffel bags in the back seat, stuffed with bundles of hundred dollar bills–which, when he had stacked them all together, had reached a height of almost 300 inches.

At 0.0043 inches thickness per bill, that meant that Derek was carrying roughly seven million dollars cash money in the back of the rented car that he was now piloting–at inadvisable speeds and with an already inadvisable and still rising blood alcohol content–away from the city he hated and towards the Mohegan Sun Casino in Uncasville, Connecticut.

The other patient that Dr. Gibbs had considered calling was still awake as well, but Maxwell Blank would also have let his voice mail pick up, since his boss disliked it when staff took calls on the job, and Maxwell was still at work.

Maxwell worked the door at Demonologie on Stuart St. in Boston, and on paper his job was simple: when a hot woman approached the club, he would unlatch the silken rope and let her in; when a plain woman approached, the rope stayed down. For men the calculus was only slightly more complicated: was the man accompanying at least one hot woman? Or was he at least dressed well enough that he might attract one? If so, up went the rope. If not: nope.

Anyone capable of applying these mindless rules could have been a passable doorman–perhaps even a good doorman–but Maxwell was a great doorman, and not only because his condition actually helped him endure the physical rigors of the job. Maxwell was a great doorman because he had the gift of making those he allowed into the club feel exclusive, while those who were denied experienced him as sympathetic but closed to appeal. He made visitors feel that the club itself, not the doorman, had decided to admit or reject them, and that–according to Maxwell's boss, who had developed his theory of "The Nightclub qua Nightclub" sufficiently that he often threatened to publish a book on the subject–was the secret to generating an aura of true exclusivity, and the highest expression of the doorman's art.

In his personal life as well Maxwell had a talent for remaining on good terms with individuals he did not admit. For example, if Maxwell were writing in his diary or speaking to Dr. Gibbs (whom by this point he treated as a kind of diary which expressed an occasional opinion on his entries) he would have asserted that he had no friends–news which would have come as a shock to the dozens of people who, in an anonymous survey, would have counted themselves as such.

Which was not to say Maxwell was a recluse. He was a social and sociable young man, rarely turning down any of the numerous invitations he received, mingling and conversing smoothly with acquaintances and strangers alike, from all walks of life, and especially with women.

He had a reputation as a boyish and earnest charmer–the kind of guy who could keep a pretty blonde giggling and tossing her hair all evening–and those who would have described themselves as Maxwell's friends assumed as a matter of course that he must be taking some percentage of these pretty blondes home. Yes, his self-described friends would have conceded, perhaps Maxwell was friendlier than he was sexual–perhaps there was something about his attitude towards clothes that suggested he could be shy about taking them off–perhaps he was not fully "comfortable in his body"–and so maybe he was not closing every deal he might have. But not a single of those self-described friends would have believed the truth: that Maxwell Blank, at 35 years of age, was still a virgin.

In theory Maxwell more or less subscribed to the three-date rule that was popular among his peers. In practice he had plenty of first dates, fewer seconds, and almost no thirds–and what third dates there were ended with him not tangled in the lady's arms and sheets but standing on her porch steps, enduring a sisterly hug or a chaste kiss on the cheek, nodding dutifully as she described that special lady who was waiting out there somewhere for Maxwell to make her deliriously happy. And those were the good third dates–the ones that did not end with the young lady excusing herself from the table to visit the restroom and never returning, or suddenly remembering a sick grandmother, roommate, or ferret that required immediate attention. Coincidentally, these young ladies always seemed to remember these invalids right after Maxwell made them aware of his condition.

According to Dr. Gibbs, Maxwell's insistence on telling a potential lover about his condition did not have its origins in chivalry, moral rectitude, or any notion of the potential lover's informed consent. As Dr. Gibbs explained it, Maxwell had an inflated sense of the significance of sexual intercourse, in that it subconsciously represented to him the installment of another woman to the post his late mother had held. Since Maxwell's mother was the only woman in the world who had been aware of his condition, therefore Maxwell–according to Dr. Gibbs–insisted that any prospective replacement must also be made aware before she could stand as a candidate for his mother's place. Maxwell had great affection for Dr. Gibbs–it was this affection that inspired him to remain Dr. Gibbs's patient, rather than any progress on his condition, as there had been none over many, many years–and he took this theory as well-meant, harmless, and rather silly.

But whether Maxwell's code of precoital honesty was written in the moral block letters that Maxwell maintained, or Dr. Gibbs's palimpsest over an Oedipal subtext, its chilling effect on his love life was not a matter of debate, and as the sympathetic hugs and kisses on the cheek piled up, Maxwell had found it increasingly difficult to regard his romantic situation with that lighthearted "right one is out there" attitude that he still professed even to his diary and psychiatrist.

He would have denied being angry with the women who had rejected him, but he could not deny that the rejections affected him. Maxwell's long-term plans for life beyond the door of Demonologie–his dreams of teaching high-school history or of opening up a kayak rental place somewhere out west–felt farther away than ever, and somehow less important, as if his condition were not just something physical, but a message from the universe–a reminder that there was no real difference between the fire of ambition and the chill acceptance of disappointment–certainly not enough of a difference that Maxwell should bother himself about it. And in his love life, such as it was, the moment of confession had begun to weigh so heavily on his mind from the first moment Maxwell met a woman that recently he was not even able to engage wholeheartedly in his normal, flirtatious conversation.

This evening for example, when the cute but slightly heavyset redhead in the coat of bright green wool and the orange skirt jogged up to the club, swinging her shoulders and puffing in the cold, his first thought was not, as it should have been, how to gently deny her entry on account of her naively cheerful fashion, thick legs, and the extra twenty pounds she was carrying–some of it in her good-natured but round face. Instead he found himself imagining how she might react if, over third-date candlelight at Icarus or L'Espalier, he confessed his condition to her. Would she be a bolter? A sobber? Would she take his hand warmly as she friendzoned him? Or would she reject him in some novel way he had never seen before? Certainly she would not profess unchanged feelings for him. Certainly she would not accept him as he was. Certainly she would not smile, warmly and openly, as she was smiling just now, as if *she* were the one greeting *him*. As a result of this moment of fantasy, Maxwell was unprepared with his normal apologetic smile and gentle speech as she approached the rope, and in his confusion he reached for a doorman's line he hadn't used in years–a rookie blunder of a line, unworthy of Maxwell's standing in his profession.

"I'm sorry, we're really full tonight."

The redhead's smile vanished and she eyed him suspiciously, but she turned to go, and for just a moment Maxwell thought he might escape unscathed–until a taxi pulled up and two underwear models stepped out. The redhead turned back around, arms crossed, and watched Maxwell with raised brows and tapping foot as he lifted the rope and let the two underwear models walk through, leaning together and giggling over a picture on one of their cell phones.

"You're really full of *something* tonight," the redhead said.

"I'm sorry," said Maxwell, "you deserved better than that."

"You mean I deserved a better rejection?"

"Wow, that was bad too–look, I'm really off my game tonight."

"Your *game*?"

"What I really meant to say was ... "

As Maxwell had no idea what he really meant to say, he was grateful to one of the valets for choosing that moment to pop out of the club.

"Hey, Maxwell," said the valet, zipping up his leather jacket, "I'm making a coffee run–you want one?"

"Yeah–actually, would you bring two? One for me and one for ... "

"I'll tell you what you can do with your coffee, *Maxwell*," said the redhead, tugging her polyester skirt to cover her knees against the cold.

"Come on, let me buy you a coffee, it's the least I can do. A coffee for me and a coffee for ... come on, a coffee for ... "

She sighed, looked over her shoulder at the cab–which was already pulling away–and turned back towards him.

"Shannon."

"For Shannon, who likes her coffee ... "

"Light and sweet. Just like you like your women, apparently."

Dr. Russell Gibbs was not in the habit of making late night phone calls, or even of being awake late enough to consider them. But he had not been able to fall asleep tonight, and he could not say why. He'd watched the late news as usual, switching off the television as that heroic theme swelled over the closing credits and shots of the Boston skyline, and then laid himself out straight on his back as always, careful not to encroach on the right half of the bed, where he kept three pillows under the blanket to imitate the form of a sleeping figure. He had not consumed more caffeine than usual, or later–just the traditional can of Diet Coke with dinner. There was nothing particular on his mind–which was to say, no more than the usual. But sleep had refused to come.

Traditionally Dr. Gibbs had been a champion sleeper, drifting off just as happily in strange surroundings as at home, or to the sounds of sirens as of silence. Even as his life had slowly fallen apart over these last years, the obsession and self-doubt that had filled the days had rarely overflown into his nights, and Dr. Gibbs had at least been able to lay head on pillow and count on seven to eight hours of blissful unconsciousness. But tonight something had bothered him and kept sleep at bay–some shadow of an idea, some whisper echoing in the back of his brain–and finally, after an hour or two of tossing and turning, he'd put on his robe and slippers and come down to the cold kitchen for a mug of hot chocolate to take into the living room. There he planned to sip and rock, sip and rock, courting sleep and watching the garden fill up with snow.

Now he stood in his kitchen, the floor so cold he could feel it through his slippers, and eyed the jar of hot chocolate with suspicion. Turning it over in his hands he read and re-read the label, hoping each time that he would find something different printed there. It was not clear to Dr. Gibbs how "stone-ground

156

chocolate" related to regular chocolate, or why it would occur to any sane individual to "blend" any kind of chocolate with "essential oils of fragrant lavender and sun-ripened chiles," and he was not sure he wanted to find out. But as this was the only option that his ransacking of the cupboard had turned up, Dr. Gibbs got some milk from the refrigerator, poured it in a saucepan, and put it to heat up on the range.

As the milk heated, Dr. Gibbs cracked the seal of the jar of hot chocolate, unscrewed the top, and sniffed at the fine powder that floated up. The nerve endings in his nostrils informed him that he had just snorted pure fire, while the taste buds nearest the back of his throat politely disagreed, opining that he had just swallowed a few well-chewed petals of lily, at least one of which had refused to descend his throat completely. It was official: his relaxing plan–with the rocking and the sipping and the snow-covered garden–had been spoiled. Yes, technically he could still go rock and watch the snow, but instead of steaming cocoa the mug would have to hold tea or decaffeinated coffee, and for Dr. Gibbs–to whom coffee tasted bitter, even with sugar and tea "dusty"–the prospect had lost a good deal of its appeal. But perhaps there was another option?

There was still, Dr. Gibbs pretended to just remember, one bottle in the house: a Balvenie 10 year that Maxwell, who couldn't have known any better, had given him three Christmases ago. Naturally Dr. Gibbs could not have thrown it away right in front of Maxwell, so he had locked it in the bottom drawer of his desk, on top of a few letters and pictures he kept from the era before Clarissa-his-ex-wife. He had fully intended to pour the contents of the bottle down the drain as soon as Maxwell's session was over, but they had run a little late that day, and Dr. Gibbs had taken no break between patients. Then, by the end of the day, Clarissa-his-ex-wife had returned home–and Dr. Gibbs was not going to open a bottle of scotch, not even to dispose of it, when she might walk into the room at any moment. After that the bottle had been forgotten until Maxwell's presence reminded him of it again–at which point Dr. Gibbs, bound by politeness, could once again take no action. And so it had gone, visit after visit, and there the bottle had stayed, until it really had been forgotten–or almost so, experienced only as a vague unease every time Clarissa-his-ex-wife had gone anywhere near the bottom drawer of his desk.

And really, where would be the harm in opening the bottle now? Dr. Gibbs was not, after all, an alcoholic. He had been an unpleasant drunk–he was man enough to admit that–as he could admit that he had come to overindulge too often. He had driven in some conditions that now shamed him to recall, and he recognized his luck in having avoided any consequences on that score. But at the very worst he had become pre-alcoholic–as someone who was eating too high on the glycemic index and neglecting exercise might become pre-diabetic. Pre-diabetes was reversible. And surely just as a recovered pre-diabetic could indulge in an ice-cream now and again, Dr. Gibbs, who was not an alcoholic, could take an occasional drink, and the world would not end.

Exhibit A: for all Clarissa-his-ex-wife's talk about groups and therapy and sponsors, when Dr. Gibbs had decided to quit drinking it had taken him not twelve steps to quit, but one: quit drinking. He had gone "cold Wild Turkey," as he had bragged to her. And he had only quit drinking at all because Clarissa-his-ex-wife had made it so clear to him that she refused to live with an alcoholic. Well, he wasn't an alcoholic–he had proven it by giving up alcohol–and she no longer lived with him anyway. So if he now decided to have a single drink, one small celebratory drink, and then did so without fuss or second-guessing or self-doubt, where would the harm be in that? Wouldn't that in fact support the fact that he was *not* an alcoholic?

The milk he had been heating for the hot chocolate interrupted this line of reasoning, foaming over the top of the pan and hissing as it reached the blue flame beneath, and Dr. Gibbs grabbed the handle without thinking. Pain shot through his hand–he dropped the pan back to the stove, where it spilled foaming milk across the entire range.

"Pot holders are next to the refrigerator, second drawer down," said a voice in his head.

"Stupid damn it stupid," Dr. Gibbs yelled to no one, certainly not to the voice in his head, whom he made it a point never to dignify with an address. He sprinted to the sink and ran cold water over his hand.

He stood holding his hand in the flow of water until it ached with cold and then felt like nothing at all, looking out through the window above the sink over the narrow strip of grass that separated his house from the neighbor's. It had stopped snowing.

As he stood there, looking out and thinking of nothing at all, Dr. Gibbs felt a sudden, almost painful event in his brain–a thought that had not been there just a moment before dropped from nowhere, fully formed, as if crystallizing from a super-saturated liquid where it had hung invisible. Dr. Gibbs understood right away that this was the idea that had kept him from sleep, but for a moment the crystalline thought sat there in the pre-language regions of his brain–he could not have expressed what he had just come to understand if he tried–and Dr. Gibbs merely continued to stand, his mouth slightly open, his hand still under the tap.

But during that moment Dr. Gibbs's mind was not idle. He could feel his Rational Agent bestir itself: put on its work boots, grab a clipboard and some coffee, a little grumpy at being roused so late, and ride down the shaft elevator to one of the deepest levels of Dr. Gibbs's subconscious–there to trudge, stooped and sweaty, through deep associations and intuitions until he reached the spot where this Big Idea had been unearthed, this potentially huge find, veined with some mythical substance that had not been seen in Dr. Gibbs's subconscious for quite some time–something called "hope."

Taking his time, so deliberate it seemed as if he were exacting revenge for the late hour, Dr. Gibbs's Rational Agent poked around, testing this "hope" at various points, pinging it with the clip of his pen and considering the resonance, shining his flashlight deep inside and peering after the beam for flaws, jotting an inscrutable note or two. Finally he looked up–as if towards a buyer waiting for a painting to be authenticated–held his pose for a theatrical interval, and nodded once. This was it. After years of failure–after so many blind alleys he did not wish to number them–Dr. Gibbs had resolved the mystery of Maxwell's condition, and of Derek's. He would call them and tell them–now, immediately–he had to.

He scrambled for the phone, not even bothering to turn off the water, and was about to dial Derek when the voice in his head started up again.

"That late news edition you watch is called the 'late news edition' because it starts at 11, right? And it lasts an hour, which makes it midnight by the time you went to bed–plus however many hours you were tossing and turning–plus however long you were looking for hot chocolate–plus however many minutes your Rational Agent just spent rummaging around the basement of your brain. Is this really the hour a respectable psychiatrist goes calling his patients? Even his last two remaining patients, with whom he's developed an unhealthy obsession that has driven everyone and everything else out of his life? Even with a 'breakthrough' like this 'Big Idea' of yours? That's assuming, by the way, that this 'Hsiao Experiment' really is a breakthrough. The details on the news report you watched seemed a little light. I know your Rational Agent put his stamp on it, but he hasn't exactly been batting 1000 recently, has he? If I were going to call Derek or Maxwell, especially at this hour, I'd want to make sure I knew what I was talking about first. But hey, I'm sure you know what you're doing. I'm sure they'll be up. I'm sure they'll be delighted to hear from you."

A moment's reflection convinced Dr. Gibbs that the voice–whom he had dubbed Clarissa-in-his-head, owing to the resemblance she shared with Clarissa-his-ex-wife in both vocabulary and views on his character–had a point. He replaced the phone on the wall.

But returning to sleep was out of the question now. If it was too late to call, he would just have to wait until morning–and in the meantime, he would grab his laptop and do some research on this "Hsiao Experiment." By the time the sun rose, he would have all his ducks in such a neat row that even Clarissa-in-his-head would have to admit that he'd cracked these cases wide open. And in the meantime, how could a celebratory sip or two go amiss? It might even take some of the sting out of his hand, which was starting to wake up again.

To Dr. Gibbs's amazement, Clarissa-in-his-head did not rebut any point of this final argument. More astonishing still, she pretended to find something interesting about her nails as he turned off the tap, wrapped a towel packed with ice around his hand, and walked to his office to retrieve his laptop and the bottle.

"Good evening sir," said the guard in the booth, "and welcome to Mohegan Sun. Could I have your name?"

"Derek Field."

The guard tapped at an iPad and swiped his finger left and right and left again across the screen, frowning.

"That's Field as in F-I-E-L-D? As in 'Field of Dreams?' "

"There a better way to spell it I've been missing?"

"Sorry?"

"That's right. 'Field of Dreams.' If you build it, I will come. You built it. Here I am."

"Sorry, sir, but I'm having a little trouble finding your reservation."

"I don't have a reservation."

"Ah–this lane is for our guests with hotel reservations."

"The sign said this was the lane for valet parking."

"Valet parking is an added service for our guests with hotel reservations only," said the guard, looking to the right, where another car had arrived and was idling behind Derek's. "But if you turn out to the left here, it'll take you to the parking garage, and you shouldn't have a problem finding the lobby and the front desk from there."

"What if you checked the list again?"

"I'm sorry sir, if you don't have a reservation, you won't be on the list."

"What if you checked the list again and I gave you 1,000 dollars?" said Derek.

"If you could just pull ... what?"

"Never mind, you had your chance. Hold on."

Derek picked up his phone from the passenger seat.

"Sir," said the guard, "there's a guest waiting behind you, I'd appreciate it if ... "

"I said hold on," said Derek to the guard. Then into his phone: "Uncasville, Connecticut. Mohegan Sun. The front desk number is fine. Oh yes, by all means connect me for an additional fee. Hello, I'd like to make a reservation. Derek Field. As in 'Field of Dreams.' Tonight. No, tonight as in technically yesterday. Yup. What's the suite situation this evening? Anything presidential left? That's the best you have?

A junior suite it is then. Now. I'm right outside. I'm going to pass you to the guy in the booth, I want you to tell him I have a reservation and qualify for valet parking."

The guard tried to wave the phone off, but Derek insisted.

"Got it," said the guard into the phone. "Yeah, you said it."

He handed the phone back to Derek.

"Valet parking is around to the right," he said as the gate lifted. "Enjoy your stay at Mohegan Sun, Mr. Field, and good luck."

The "good luck" part irked Derek even more than the rest of his experience, and for a moment he wished he hadn't sold the BMW so he could have revved the engine and peeled through the gate. Instead he drove through slowly, and even resisted the urge to comment a moment later when the valet's eyes widened with disapproval at the six empty cans in the passenger seat.

Better to get even than mad. So if things went terribly wrong tonight, he would use the winnings to buy this whole beautiful casino. He would fire everyone who worked there, one by one–starting with the idiot in the booth and this judgy valet–and then he'd burn the whole place to the ground and roast marshmallows over the cinders. And then and only then would he put the bullet in his brain.

"It's a simple question," Shannon said. She wrapped her hands around the cardboard cup in the hopes that some warmth still remained from her long-finished coffee, and then gave up, tossing it into the can at Maxwell's side and thrusting her hands in the pockets of her green coat.

"Are you cold?" asked Maxwell.

"Of course I'm cold. Answer the question."

"Do you want my coat?"

"I don't want your coat, I want an answer to the question."

"A robot could definitely lift the rope," said Maxwell. "Here, take the coat."

"Yeah, not interested in that part of your job–I want to know if a robot could decide who to let in. And for the last time, I don't want your damn coat."

"I don't really know anything about robots."

"But you're the world expert on deciding who to let into Demonologie. Robots have to work on some kind of rules or formula, right? So is there a simple formula you could program into a robot?"

"It's stopped snowing," said Maxwell, "I really don't need my coat."

"Stop changing the subject, if I cared about the snow and cold I wouldn't be standing out here. I want to know whether or not you think a robot could decide who to let in to Demonologie."

"Can we talk about something else?"

"Because you think I'll be offended by what you say, since you didn't let me in?"

"Because I let in 'hot' women, just like my boss told me to. It's that simple, and it's not that interesting."

"But you have to decide if a woman is hot, and there's nothing simple about that," said Shannon. "I studied art, and it's incredibly hard to define any aesthetic–let alone an aesthetique like Demonologie's. Take this fine specimen who's walking up right now.

What's going on in your mind? Is it like" (she made her voice flat and robotic) "loading brunette program … detecting cosmetically enhanced, haunted eyes … check … detecting dress size less than or equal to eight … check … detecting evidence of recent salon trip … check … hotness confirmed. Have a great time in there tonight," she said in answer to the passing woman's look, keeping the voice of a cheerful robot greeter.

Maxwell smiled in apology as he lifted the rope for the brunette, glaring at Shannon over her shoulder as she passed.

"You're going to get me fired," he said. "So where did you study art?"

"And you're a slow learner–you're not getting out of this by changing the subject. Was I right with the robot thing? You have like, a checklist of measurements and features, and if she meets some minimum score she's hot and you let her in?"

"No, I don't have a checklist."

"Then it's subjective?"

"Those are my choices–checklist or subjective?"

"Yes."

"Then I guess it's subjective, because I definitely don't have a checklist."

"So what you're really saying is that you let in the women you're attracted to, and keep out the ones you're not attracted to."

"Hold on just a second," said Maxwell. "Judging whether a woman is 'hot' doesn't mean just asking myself whether or not I'm attracted to her. I'm deciding on behalf of the club."

"The 'club' is a building, or maybe a business, but either way it doesn't find anyone attractive. Watch this."

Shannon sidled up to the building, doing her best to toss her short hair, and reached out to touch the concrete wall.

"Hey baby," she said, and waited. "You see? Nothing. Just cold stone."

"OK, then I'm deciding in the best interests of the club as a business–which means, I guess, that I'm trying to judge whether the majority of our clientele–specifically our male clientele, which buys the drinks in there–would find a woman attractive. It has nothing to do with my own tastes: there are plenty of women I let in who I'm not personally attracted to, and there are plenty of women I can't let in who I find very attractive and would totally go out with."

"Maxwell," said Shannon sweetly, as he unlatched the rope to admit a six foot Amazon whose cold-weather outerwear could have graced the pages of a Victoria's Secret catalog, "are you asking me out on a date?"

Even calling this horrific violation of basic human rights an 'experiment' is an insult to the scientific method. An experiment isolates a single variable and tests its effect on another variable. An experiment does not permit multiple interpretations. An experiment can be replicated. So by the generally agreed definition of 'experiment,' even the crackpot notion of quantum suicide could never fit the bill, or be worthy of scientific notice, let alone quantum execution.

"And that's just one commenter on CNN.com who happens to know the tiniest bit about science," said Clarissa-in-his-head. "Imagine what the real scientists will have to say."

The second and third scotches had gone down very nicely, and Dr. Gibbs decided to answer her, as he almost never did. He even spoke out loud.

"You take such pleasure seeing holes poked in my theory, just because it's *my* theory. What about Derek and Maxwell? Don't you have any sympathy for them?"

"Don't pretend you're motivated by Maxwell and Derek's well being."

"Pretend? I'll have you know that every morning for almost forty years, before my first session of the day, I would look at myself in the mirror and remind my reflection 'We are here to end human suffering.' I'd say it over and over–some mornings 50 times–until I could see that the reflection understood me–that I really felt the enormity of what I was saying. At a cocktail party Oliver Sacks once called me ..."

"A humanist of Renaissance proportions, yes I remember. You excused yourself to the bathroom where you got all choked up."

"How did you know that? I never told anyone that part."

"I'm in your head, remember? You got into psychiatry with noble intentions, I believe that, I always have. But you lost them somewhere along the way–somewhere between your book and your obsession with Maxwell and Derek. How exactly are you helping those two? Maxwell manages his condition just fine. Derek has farther to go, but at least he's still in the ring, wrestling with his demons. They're the ones with the problems, Russell, but you're the one who's drowning. You've lost your practice, your wife, and now you've lost your battle with the bottle. Are you saying this helped them somehow? That you lost all this for them? That you're investigating this insane 'experiment' for them?"

Dr. Gibbs poured himself another scotch and sat for a few minutes, nursing it.

"Yes. No. I can't tell any more," he said finally. "When Maxwell came to me, I was okay. You remember that. I was mystified, but it was just one case. It was like that one story that everyone has on tap for a cocktail party, the one thing they've seen in their life that's impossible to explain. Lights in the sky or footsteps in an empty house. Spice of life stuff. These are the weird exceptions that prove the rule of normalcy, right? And he seemed to take it in such stride himself. He was never looking for answers about his condition–he just wanted to learn how to live his life despite it.

"But then Derek arrived, and I could feel something about him from the beginning. What he was saying was crazy, but he didn't sound crazy when he said it. That was unsettling. Right away he wanted to demonstrate the Curse to me, to prove it was real, and I was afraid to let him. I should have listened to those fears–because once he showed me, it wasn't just a cocktail story, and neither was Maxwell. Derek was like the plane hitting the second tower. I understood that this was no accident–it was an attack. My trust in a rational universe was under attack."

Dr. Gibbs stopped to pour another finger's worth of scotch.

"I never told you this story, but at one point I started to wonder if all psychiatrists had such cases, and it was just a point of professional honor not to talk about them–some concession to public mental health. Maybe I just hadn't gotten the memo. So at a convention in Denver, sitting at the bar–I was only drinking ginger ale–after a long conversation with one Dr. Sutherland, I finally worked up the courage to ask. Did he have any *special* patients? What did I mean by that, he asked? Well, patients that you wouldn't really talk about at all, even anonymized, even in papers. Patients you thought it was better people didn't even know about. He became extremely awkward and left the bar, claiming an upset stomach.

"Six months later he sent me a letter. It wasn't on letterhead. He didn't know how I'd known about the patient he was sleeping with, but he thanked me for challenging him about it so tactfully. After our chat he had done some real soul searching, which had led to his terminating the relationship and closing his practice. He'd lost his livelihood but regained his integrity. His wife had decided to stand by him. Things weren't easy but they were working it out. He was opening a restaurant and hoped to 'do some good through food.' He had never for a moment understood what I was really talking about. So I knew: these things weren't happening to everyone. Just to me."

Dr. Gibbs stopped speaking and closed his eyes. He could almost hear his wife breathing near him.

"It feels good to talk to you about these things. I'm not a bad man, you know, Clarissa. I'm just ... what am I?"

"Do you remember the night you brought me up to the roof of your dorm, and had beers and Indian food waiting?" asked Clarissa-in-his-head.

"Of course I do. It was our third date."

"I made you a promise that night. Do you remember it?"

"You promised me that you would always tell me the truth, even if it was uncomfortable to say or to hear. And then you told me you hated Indian food."

"With a passion ... "

"As hot as a Vindaloo curry."

"I kept that promise over our years together. And I'll keep it now. You're *not* a bad man, Russell. You're just in over your head. You thought that all it took to be a good man was to think no evil, not of others or of yourself. Then life pulled the rug out from under you. I understand–you weren't equipped for that, and I didn't know how to help you. But you have a good heart. You said a minute ago that you didn't even know any more whose interests you were acting in by investigating the Hsiao Experiment–Derek and Maxwell's or your own. You've tangled yourself up with them, and them with each other, so that if one of you goes under, you all drown. On the other hand, you think that if somehow you manage to keep all three of you afloat, you'll have vindicated the sacrifice of everything else in your life: your other patients, your own health. Me."

"You," he said out loud.

The radiator hissed and clanged. Dr. Gibbs opened his eyes. His laptop had gone to sleep. He shook the mouse to wake it up, took off his glasses to rub the bridge of his nose, and, as Clarissa-in-his-head fell quiet again, began to re-read the Wikipedia article on quantum suicide.

"Yes, you can help me with something," said Derek into the hotel phone, meanwhile shaking his finger to prevent the bellhop from leaving. "You've given me a non-smoking room. I need a smoking room. No, I don't want to smoke on the gaming floor, or outside–I need a smoking room. Yeah, try that and call me back."

Derek hung up.

"Want to bet whether she's going to call back or not?"

"If there's nothing else, Mr. Field," said the valet.

"Yeah, one more thing. How do I disable the smoke detector in the bathroom?"

"Tampering with the smoke detectors is a violation of Connecticut law. Many of our bars and gaming areas welcome smokers, or you are always welcome to step outside the building." The valet recited these words–identical to the ones the woman at the front desk had just used–like a hostage reading from cue cards held by his captors. He had a thin face and prominent forehead and chin, and a caricaturist might have rendered him as a freckled banana, or a crescent moon with marijuana eyes. He looked to be about college age.

"Saving for school?" said Derek.

"What?"

Derek threw one of the duffel bags on the bed and pulled out ten $100 bills from a rubber-banded stack.

The bills were so crisp that he had to rub them between his finger and thumb to unstick them from each other.

"I don't want to tamper with the smoke detector, I want to turn it off. Help me out," he said, and slapped the bills against his palm with a practiced motion–the bellhop jumped at the sharpness of the crack.

"You can totally disable the smoke detector," said the bellhop, in his normal, non-hostage voice. "Actually, I can do it for you."

"I certainly would appreciate that," said Derek.

As the bellhop climbed up on the sink, Derek took a look around the "junior suite," opening the curtains and peering out into the blackness that was supposed to be the river view. He stopped in front of the mini-bar and picked up a couple nips, reading the labels before replacing them.

"Oh, man, you don't want to do that," said the valet, wiping his hands on his pants as he emerged from the bathroom. "They've got weight sensors on the mini-bar, they'll totally charge you for anything you pick up, even if you don't drink it. I can take care of that for you downstairs, though, no problem."

"Don't worry about it," said Derek, picking up a tiny bottle of tequila and opening it. "Thanks for your help with the smoke detector."

He folded the bills once and handed them over.

"Yeah, no problem," said the valet. "We smokers got to hang together, right? Fight the power? Hey," he added when he was already out the door, "do you think I could bum a cig?"

"Sorry," said Derek, "I don't smoke."

He closed the door and engaged the bolt.

Once he was alone, Derek sat down on the bed. He stretched over, hauled the second duffel bag up, and unzipped it. Tenderly, almost reverently, he removed the one object in the bag that was not money–a well-loved copy of *The Suffering Decision*, by Dr. Russell Gibbs–and, standing and pulling a lighter from his pocket, walked towards the bathroom.

Maxwell tried the door of the club to make sure it was locked.

"So where do you want to go?" Shannon asked.

"We don't have a ton of options. There's a 24 hour diner where I get pancakes sometimes after work. You like pancakes?"

"Who doesn't like pancakes?"

"It's going to be hard to get a cab, with all the clubs closing. We can walk–it's just a few blocks–or if you're too cold, you can wait in the club while I get a cab."

"I've been standing outside with you for hours, Maxwell. I think I can handle walking a few blocks. Although it might be nice to finally get a peek inside Demonologie."

She spoke this last sentence with obvious good humor, but Maxwell still found himself looking at his shoes.

"Shall we?" she said.

They set off, leaving their footprints in the layer of fresh snow.

It was strange, Maxwell thought, how quickly they fell into an awkward silence after so many hours of banter. It was as if a man and woman walking to dine together represented an unusual happening, so novel that no conventions had yet accrued around it–while a woman who had been denied entrance to a club milling around for hours with the very man who had denied her entrance had seemed the most natural situation in the world, and an occasion for easy conversation.

As they stepped over a frozen puddle half a block from the diner–the lighted windows were already visible–Shannon took Maxwell's arm.

"Mmmm," she said. "You're so warm."

She must have felt his arm stiffen under his jacket, because she let go right away.

"You know, if you'd rather just call it a night, that's fine," she said. "We can pick this up another time, or whatever."

As she spoke a cab passed by, and the two frat boys in the back rolled down the window and hooted at them. Shannon gave them the finger.

"No, I wouldn't," said Maxwell. "I really wouldn't. I'm sorry if I'm acting a little strange, but–look, I don't even usually bring this up until date three, but you seem really cool, and I'm just wondering if I really want to get my hopes up when you're just going to freak out when you find out anyway."

"You're kind of in danger of freaking me out right now, Maxwell," said Shannon.

"I know, I'm sorry. The worst part is, it's not really that big a deal. But I have this condition–it's actually really dumb. It's nothing dangerous or catching, but it's just this thing that ... "

At the word "condition," something seemed to click inside Shannon. She put a finger up to his lips, and Maxwell trailed off in confusion.

"Tell you what: let's take the pressure off, shall we? We don't even have to call this a date. We're just two people eating pancakes. We'll go Dutch as a Rembrandt. But we're already here. I can smell the pancakes–they smell pretty damn good, and I'm starving. And furthermore, I'm freezing my ass off. So why don't we sit down where it's warm, fortify ourselves with some coffee and a couple full stacks with butter and maple syrup, and then, if you still want to, you can tell me all about it?"

With her finger still on his lips Maxwell didn't speak, but he nodded once. When they resumed walking, Shannon did not, as he had hoped she would, take his arm again.

Dr. Gibbs woke up slowly at first, realizing in stages that, just as in his dream, he was pouring from a bottle of scotch, but that–unlike in his dream–he was pouring it not into a cut-glass tumbler but onto the keyboard of his laptop. The fatigue and lingering effects of the scotch sent him into a spasm of response, and he started twice from his chair to fetch a towel before he even thought to stop pouring. As quickly as he could he put the bottle down on the desk and unplugged the A/C power from the the back of the laptop, but he still lacked the presence of mind to remember the battery, or to understand for a few seconds why the laptop refused to shut off. Somewhere behind the keyboard something popped and fizzled, and the screen went blank.

Dr. Gibbs leaned back in his chair, defeated. The bottle was almost empty. Scotch had pooled beneath his laptop and was dripping off the desk and onto his robe and slippers.

He groaned and shook his head, face in hands, perhaps mourning the waste of so much fine liquor, or the negligent destruction of an expensive piece of technology, or the moment of weakness that had ended his five years sober–or perhaps the fact that he was facing all of these minor tragedies alone, in an empty house that was not large but was too large for just him, while somewhere beneath bright New Hampshire stars Clarissa-his-ex-wife slumbered sweetly beside Don the Handsome Salesman of Insurance, dreaming of who knew what, but certainly not of Dr. Gibbs. His head hurt and he could not catch his breath. He did not even attempt to wipe up the scotch–it was simply impossible to face this disaster until morning.

Dr. Gibbs groped and stumbled blindly up to the bedroom. There was something else that he should do before he fell asleep. Brush his teeth? Lock the door? But these could wait. The warmth of the bed was impossibly inviting as he fell in, shoes and all.

"Did you check the stove to make sure the gas was off?" asked Clarissa-in-his-head.

"You used to ask me that every night," he said out loud, reaching for the pillow next to him.

Derek struck the lighter, and an almond-shaped flame danced in the draft of the bathroom fan. *The Suffering Decision* lay face up in the sink, curving at the edges of the bowl like a man trying to sleep in a bathtub. Derek had first placed the book face down, as if sparing a condemned man from the sight of his executioner, but he could not bring open flame towards the portrait of Dr. Gibbs on the rear cover and had been forced to flip the book over.

That picture must have been taken at least ten years ago–Dr. Gibbs's face was thinner than Derek had ever seen it, and his hair and beard still showed some pepper mixed in with the salt. He was smiling in front of his garden, wearing a straw hat and leaning on a hoe or rake. His cheeks were dappled with sun. Derek suspected that his wife had snapped the photo.

Derek would not have described his feelings towards Dr. Gibbs as a son's feelings towards a father, but that was due more to a lack of relevant experience–almost a lack of vocabulary–than any lack of emotion. Derek had exactly one memory of his father: a round, bearded face aglow with the light of what Derek had deduced to be between 25 and 27 candles inclusive, sucking in the breath to blow them out.

His father looked happy in this memory, and over time he had grown to look happier, as if he were slowly realizing just how delicious a chocolate cake from a Duncan Hines mix could actually be, or as if the memory were itself conscious, gradually accruing an older man's understanding of just how good it actually was to be 25 to 27 years of age inclusive, blowing out the candles on the birthday cake your wife had made you, forever.

In some of their earlier sessions Dr. Gibbs had made noises about Derek's forgiving his father being an important step in breaking the Curse, but–to Derek's relief–he had given that idea up. There was no world in which Derek could forgive his father for deserting his mother and himself, not because the hurt was too deep, or because Derek was not a forgiving person, but because he felt no injury to forgive. Derek had never known his father. He had never been tempted to track him down and seek his approval, and–not being skilled at or interested in hypotheticals–he had no concept of what life might have been like if his father had been present through it. His father had done injury not to Derek but to the notion of fatherhood, and it seemed to Derek that to absolve him would require not Derek's forgiveness, but the forgiveness of every father's son everywhere. It would have been like collecting signatures door to door.

Whereas Derek forgave Dr. Gibbs without even noticing that he was doing so: forgave him for misguided notions like the above, for the professional arrogance that occasionally broke through, for his initial refusal to believe in the Curse and his continued inability to break it. Derek even forgave Dr. Gibbs for the failures and unhappiness in Dr. Gibbs's own life (the weight the psychiatrist had still not stopped gaining, the increasingly unkempt beard, the loss of his wife–whose footsteps Derek never heard above anymore during sessions–as well as the rest of his practice).

Or nearly the rest of his practice. There was someone else who still came to visit Dr. Gibbs–Derek could feel his presence. Dr. Gibbs asked patients to arrive at the front door and exit through the back, and on occasion Derek would hear the front door close as he opened the back, or vice versa. He had never seen the young man–for some reason Derek assumed that he was a young man–but he felt a kinship with him, as if their destinies were entangled, as if they were bound together by their mutual association with Dr. Gibbs. Derek had even begun to feel, or at least imagine, that the young man was crossing paths with him elsewhere: stepping off a subway just as Derek stepped on, or riding down the elevator adjacent to the one in which Derek was ascending.

The flame was still dancing–the lighter had grown hot in Derek's hand.

"This is ridiculous," he said out loud. "One book can't possibly count for the Curse."

Lifting his thumb off the plunger, he threw the lighter into the trash and retrieved the book from the sink. He tossed it in the top drawer of the bedside table, right next to the Gideon Bible, and slammed the drawer shut.

Then, one duffel bag in each hand, Derek headed out the door and down to the gaming floor.

"Mmm," said Shannon, taking her first bite, "I like the little crispiness they get on these things. You, sir, have good taste in pancakes."

The only other customers in the diner–a pair of drunk female club-goers–had paid their bill and stumbled out, giggling, before Maxwell and Shannon had even received their coffee. They were alone now except for the bored waitress who sat behind the counter, watching a mute presentation of *The Princess Bride* on the television mounted in the corner.

"So what do you do?" asked Maxwell.

"Ugh."

"Your job's that bad?"

"No, I mean 'ugh' that we're at the 'so what do you do' part of the evening. I thought there were more interesting things we were going to talk about?"

"All I really know about you is that you studied art and have a disturbing knack for cutting through my BS. I'd like to know a little more before spilling my guts."

"All right," said Shannon, "time me, I'm going for the record. Ready? Born near Chicago–parents both teachers–one sister, older, yes we get along–hated school until college–studied art–tried painting, tried sculpting, accepted my own artistic mediocrity–now work as a graphic designer. Hobbies include fixing old cars and getting denied entrance to chic nightclubs. Time! How fast was I?"

"I'm never going to live the club down, am I?"

"Actually I don't mind. Really I hate clubs. But I do like to dance, and clubs are the only place to do that."

"So is that your dream job?"

"Dancing?" she said. "Maybe–I'd never considered it as a career."

"No, graphic design."

"I guess so. That doesn't make it sound like it's my dream job, does it? Don't get me wrong, I like graphic design. It's just that when I was younger I had this crazy idea that I'd be some kind of problem solver–maybe because I was obsessed with Encyclopedia Brown. You remember him?"

"Of course. So you wanted to grow up to be a boy detective?"

"You're hilarious. No, I had this vision that I'd be in an office with, like, a plant, a window, and a database, and people would come to me with their problems, and I'd help them."

"What kind of plant?"

"Either a fern or a ficus. I haven't decided yet. So is working the door at Demonologie your dream job?"

"I want to hear more about this plant and window and database."

"At some point," said Shannon, pointing her fork at him, "you're going to have to say something about yourself. If I recall, there was some 'condition' you were going to tell me about once I had my pancakes and coffee, which–let me check–yep, I've definitely got."

"I don't know if that was such a great idea. Another time."

"Come on, Max. You can't get lucky unless you roll the dice."

"I'm worried this is more like pulling the trigger in Russian roulette."

He made no more response until, after a few more bites of pancake, Shannon looked up at him, widening her eyes and making two circles in the air with her fork. The fluorescent light caught a ginger hair on her arm.

Maxwell remembered the possibilities he had envisioned upon first seeing her as she jogged up to the door of Demonologie–the outright bolting, the false warmth, the concerned hand-hold, the undisguised, derisive laugh. In none of the eventualities he'd imagined had she looked like this, open and warm and matter-of-fact, urging him with her fork to come clean. For that matter, none of the women he'd confessed to had ever looked remotely like that either–even the kindest of them had been unable to hide discomfort around what he might be about to reveal.

"All right," he said, riding this sudden wave of hope before it could dissipate and allow intelligent self-preservation to reassert control, "what the hell."

"In the room is a large wooden box with a door on one side. You enter the box alone, closing the door behind you. Inside there is only a bare bulb providing light, a trigger attached to the front wall and, mounted on the back wall, a gun.

"Pulling the trigger will activate a device to measure some quantum state–let us say, whether a certain electron has an up spin or a down spin. If the spin is up, nothing will happen. If the spin is down, the gun fires a bullet. I neglected to mention that the gun has been carefully positioned so that the bullet will fire into your brain, killing you instantly.

"You walk up to the trigger, take a deep breath, and pull it. What happens to you now depends on which dead white male with the European name was smarter–Werner Heisenberg or Erwin Schrödinger."

The laughter that rippled through the conference room was more than polite, which pleased Dr. Gibbs. Eventually he had to raise his hand to stop it.

"If Heisenberg is right you are just flipping a coin–in the form of measuring an electron–and have a fifty-fifty chance of living or dying. According to him the quantum uncertainty about whether the electron's spin is up or down is not an uncertainty in the nature of the universe, but in the *measurement* of the universe. Observations at quantum scale are just so difficult that they can only be described as probabilities. This is the so-called Copenhagen Interpretation, named for the city in which Heisenberg proposed it.

"But if Schrödinger is right–and the uncertainty in quantum theory reflects not the difficulty of measuring quantum-sized events, but an actual fuzziness in the fabric of reality–then a far stranger fate befalls you. In the instant you pull that trigger the universe splits in two. In one universe, the spin of the electron is down, and you are killed instantly. In the other, the spin of the electron is up, and you survive.

"Now in the universe where the gun went off, you will not be aware–because you will be dead. You will only be aware in the universe where you have survived, where you will think that you just got lucky–that the spin of the electron just happened to be up. But consider what happens now if you–or to be more precise, the 'you' who was fortunate enough to survive in the universe with the up-spinning electron–pulls the trigger again.

"The universe splits again, and you with it. Again, one of you dies, unaware, and one survives, aware. Another pull on the trigger–yet another universe. And again, and again. In fact, ladies and gentlemen, if Schrödinger is right and the Copenhagen Interpretation wrong, you will be able to pull that trigger as many times as you like–or until your nerve runs out–and the 'you' that survives will experience nothing worse than the repeated clicking of the trigger–and, perhaps, some very understandable anxiety."

More laughter.

"The thought experiment we have just described was originally proposed by another man with a

184

European name–the futurist and technologist Hans Moravec–in 1987, as a method for disproving the Copenhagen Interpretation. He called his method 'quantum suicide.' Yes, there's a question in the first row?"

"Dr. Paul Sutherland, Yale University. So if I'm following you, quantum suicide–if it worked–could disprove the Copenhagen Interpretation to the subject in the box, since he only experiences the parallel universes in which he survives. But the subject is also leaving behind other universes in which he dies–and in those universes, the people outside the box hear a bang and run in to find him dead. So they'll still believe that the Copenhagen Interpretation is true, no?"

"An astute observation, Dr. Sutherland, and absolutely correct. Which leads us to the Hsiao Experiment, named for Liyan Hsiao, warden of the Tilanqiao Prison in Shanghai, the largest prison in China, and–when he took over–the most overpopulated."

"23 red."

"Yes!" shouted Derek. He pumped his fist and turned to the old woman sitting next to him.

"That right there," he said, pointing at the stack of chips the croupier pushed his way, "is how baby gets new shoes."

She smiled politely, gathered up her own chips, and went to find another table. She had been the last holdout–Derek now found himself alone, which suited him fine. He hummed a few bars of "Sussudio" as he stacked his winnings and prepared his next bet.

"How we doing this evening, sir?" said the man behind him.

Derek had not heard or seen the man approach–it was as if he had materialized there, and was now hovering just behind Derek's left shoulder at the distance a tailor might maintain–measuring tape still around his shoulders–allowing a customer enough range of motion to test an adjustment while never letting him forget that the tailor was still in charge of his movements. Two other men stood further behind, arms folded, at about the same distance again.

The man was short–perhaps five foot six–and almost as wide as he was tall. He wore his hair buzzed to the skull. An awkwardly placed scar, visible only when the light caught it, sloped very low across his cheek and chin, as if he'd been on the wrong end of a broken bottle in a bar fight. But he radiated a friendly and cheerful energy.

"What's the problem?" Derek asked, turning back to his chips.

"There's no problem, Mr. ... "

"Field. As in 'Field of Dreams,' as in the dream that I'm living right now. Oh *yeah*! Seventeen on the nose!"

"There's no problem at all, Mr. Field.   I'm Mr. Esposito. I work for the casino."

"No shit?"

"Let me buy you a drink in the bar."

"I can get a drink at the table. I'm on a hot streak, and you never walk away from the table on a hot streak."

"Well that's the problem, Mr. Field ... "

"So there *is* a problem."

"Ha, I like that. You're a sharp one, Mr. Field. You'd get along with my wife. What I mean is, that's the *thing* I'd like to chat about–your hot streak."

"You're not suggesting that I'm cheating?" said Derek, a little louder than he had intended.

A young inebriated couple who had been scouting seats at the end of the table seemed to change their minds and staggered onward.

"Give me five minutes," said Mr. Esposito. "You can leave your chips here, I'll make sure nobody touches them. I'm still asking, but the thing is ..." he paused, nodding over his shoulder to the two men behind him, "... I don't *have* to ask."

Derek examined the other two men, neither of whom seemed to share Mr. Esposito's pudgy physique or his fundamental good cheer. One of them rolled his shoulders and worked his neck from side to side.

"Five minutes," said Derek, "and my bags come with me."

"Of course. You ever had a Sazerac?" asked Mr. Esposito, as they walked off the floor and into a wolf-den themed bar only a few steps away. At a nod from him, his two compatriots did not follow. "It's different. From New Orleans. The original cocktail, they say. Our bartender here makes them the best. Well, to be completely honest with you, I've never had one anywhere else, but these are pretty damn good. Bert, get me and Mr. Field a couple Sazeracs."

Derek did not protest.

"Look, Mr. Field," said Mr. Esposito as Bert got busy with the cocktails, "I want nothing more than to let you play in peace, but your behavior is making that hard for me. You're spooking our other guests–you cleared out that whole table. I even heard a couple people walking away talking about things like the odds of the game and the house edge, and–I'm going to be painfully frank with you–those are details we prefer our guests don't think about."

"I can't control what your other guests say or do."

"But can you control what *you* say and do?"

"Maybe I got a little excited once or twice. My bad. I'll rein it in. But I don't understand why a man can't get a little excited when his roulette system is working. First no smoking, now no celebrating. Is this a library or a casino? Or should I just head across the river to Foxwoods? Is that what you're saying?"

"By all means, get a little excited when you win. We love that, it's all part of the Mohegan Sun experience. But–there's really no delicate way to put this to you, I'm just going to say it–your system isn't working. You're not winning."

"I haven't blanked on a spin all night."

"You're hitting the spin, but you're losing money. I don't mean in the 'house always wins eventually' way–I mean you're losing money on each and every spin of the wheel. You're betting every square every time, Mr. Field. That's not gambling–that's absolutely 100 percent guaranteed to lose. You seem like a smart guy–you have to see how that's not going to work out for you."

"It's working out for me just fine."

"Okay, forget the big bets you're tossing around, I'll make this simple: let's say you put a dollar on every square, 1 through 36, and both the zeroes. That's 38 dollars. Whatever number comes up, you're going to win 35 bucks back, plus your original bet. That's 36 dollars. You just won 36 dollars on 38 ventured. You're down two bucks on every spin. It's mathematically guaranteed."

"Isn't it fantastic? The system is perfect."

"See, that's the kind of remark that's weirding our guests out, and me too. I don't understand what you're getting at."

"You don't have to understand, Mr. Esposito."

"Still, I'd be grateful if you could make me understand."

"Two Sazeracs," said Bert, depositing the highball glasses on the bar. The liquid inside was a rusty color, not at all like the bright green that Derek had imagined from the name, and the frosty glass felt good on his fingers as he picked it up. He realized that he had been sweating since Mr. Esposito had appeared behind him.

"You want to understand my thinking?" said Derek, pausing to take a sip of the Sazerac–it tasted like licorice. "All right, what the hell. You have a coin handy? You flip, I call. You good for a dollar a toss?"

"In sixth grade," Maxwell said, "when I was twelve, right in the middle of January, some jerk super-glued my locker shut."

"Did you know who it was?" said Shannon.

"I'm pretty sure I know who it was–I was too scared to rat, though. But the point is, my coat was in that locker, and I was too ashamed to tell anyone what had happened, so in the middle of January I walked home without it, wearing just a t-shirt."

"Uphill in the snow?"

"What?"

"Both ways?"

"Ah, right. Actually, it was uphill going home, but it wasn't snowing–it was too cold to snow that day. From school to my house was almost two miles, and all these cars would slow down as they passed me. I could see worried mothers peering through their windshields, waving and trying to get my attention. A bunch stopped and offered me a ride. One woman was so insistent that I had to run down a side street to get away from her."

"Why didn't you just take a ride?"

"My mom–may she rest in peace–was pretty big on my not talking to strangers."

"She'd rather have you freeze to death?"

"Hold that thought. So finally I got home, and I tried to sneak in the house without my mother seeing me coatless, but she happened to be right there when I came in. She totally lost it. Why hadn't I called her, why hadn't I gone to the office, or borrowed a jacket, I was going to catch my death, all that stuff, and meanwhile I'm trying to calm her down by telling her that I wasn't cold–which was true."

"After a two mile walk in sub-zero temps? With only a t-shirt?"

"Her objection precisely. So she drags me upstairs, still flipping out, and fills the bathtub with water you could steam a lobster in, and leaves me to it, but she's screaming through the door to lower myself in gently, and when she hears me plop in all at once she loses the shred of sanity she's been clinging to and bursts into the bathroom."

"And you were twelve? That must have been a traumatic experience. Is your condition that you're unable to bathe without symptoms of PTSD? Because I would understand."

"Yeah, even though I live alone now I lock the bathroom door religiously. But anyway, after a bunch of screaming back and forth, and her trying to pull me out of the water, and me trying to cover myself with a towel, she starts to get it–that I should be shivering from the walk home, but I'm not–that I should be screaming in pain from the bath, but I'm not–and I finally manage to convince her that I really can't feel the scalding water–just like I couldn't feel the cold outside. And thus began my march through an army of doctors and specialists."

Shannon put down her fork and looked at him.

"That's it? Maxwell, I have to be honest: you had me hoping for something more twisted and exotic. I thought maybe you needed chicken blood transfusions twice a week, or you had a miniature conjoined twin in your abdomen who was going to pop out at some point, like 'Heeeere's Johnny!' Now *those* would be conditions. You've just got that thing where you can't feel hot and cold? Can you feel pain?"

"There are a bunch of such things: CIPA, Riley Day Syndrome. Thermoanesthesia. But I don't have any of them. I feel pain just like anyone else, and I can probably feel hot and cold just fine too."

"You just told me a long story about how you *couldn't* feel them."

"Do you have a lighter?"

"I don't smoke."

"That's not what I asked."

"Why do you want my lighter?"

"Pass it over."

"First tell me why."

"If you don't give it to me, I'll just get some matches from the waitress."

"Be careful," said Shannon. "My cousin gave me this–it's my good luck charm."

Maxwell took the reluctantly proffered lighter–a well worn Zippo with a Grateful Dead logo on the side. After two tries it struck. He transferred the lighter to his left hand with a theatrical slowness, and–avoiding Shannon's eyes–placed his right index finger directly into the flame. He held it there.

"Stop that," said Shannon. "Maxwell, stop it. I said *stop!*"

She reached over the table and batted the lighter out of his hand. It skittered across the tile floor of the diner, stopping near the foot of the waitress, who had just been heading in the direction of their table to check on their coffee situation, but now thought better of it.

"I'll get that," Maxwell said.

"Shut up and give me your hand," said Shannon, fishing some ice from her water and wrapping it in a clean napkin. "You idiot."

"Shannon, it's fine."

"Give me your hand."

"No, look," said Maxwell, holding up the finger he had been cooking. "I don't mean that it doesn't hurt. I mean it's fine."

"Six months after Hsiao took over Tilanqiao," said Dr. Gibbs, "it was still the largest prison in China, but no longer the most overcrowded. This achievement, if you want to call it that, was due to

192

Hsiao's 'Scientific Overcrowding Relief Initiative'–a whitewashed, bureaucratic term for the practice of building a quantum suicide box and forcing a stream of inmates to enter it and pull the trigger 100 times each."

Dr. Gibbs paused to make sure the horror of this statement had sunk in, but it was difficult to make out individual faces in the audience.

"By all accounts Hsiao did not consider the practice either an experiment or a pretext for execution. A true believer in parallel universes, he saw the 'initiative' as a cutting-edge application of quantum physics to the real-world problem of prison overcrowding. He believed that, by sending prisoners to their deaths in this fashion, he was merely shuffling that prisoner's consciousness into other universes, in which they survived unharmed. At his trial he argued that every prisoner he ever sent into the box, from the prisoner's point of view, had suffered no ill effects, merely exiting the box 100 trigger pulls later, none the worse for wear, to serve out the remainder of his sentence in a facility that the party–at least the party in *this* universe–did not have to pay for.

"It is not clear how much the broader government knew, and when, about what Hsiao was doing. Of course the official statements from the party have consisted of nothing but denials of any involvement and blanket assertions that Hsiao acted alone. But Hsiao was recognized twice in two years for improving the numbers in Tilanqiao, and other prisons even shipped him prisoners–by some accounts as many as 20,000–in order to ease their own overcrowding.

"To this day we might not have heard anything about Hsiao's practice if it weren't for the guard who released the videotapes of a number of prisoners actually entering the boxes–including the single prisoner who survived all 100 trigger-pulls. Yes, in the front row?"

"Dr. Wilbur Mayberry, Harvard University. I understand that a number of people–yourself included perhaps–interpret this lone survivor as proof of parallel universes. But if Hsiao put so many prisoners through the box–50,000 was the number I heard–weren't one or two bound to survive?"

"Dr. Mayberry, do you have any idea how slim the odds are of anyone surviving 100 trigger pulls? Far slimmer than one in 50,000. The actual number is one in two to the hundredth, which is, let's see: 2, 4, 8, 16, 32 ... "

"That's 100 even," said Derek.

"Impossible," said Mr. Esposito. "Can't happen."

"Did happen. So it's not impossible–just very unlikely."

"So unlikely it's impossible."

"Do you happen to know the exact odds of winning 100 coin flips in a row?" Derek asked. "I do–it's kind of a bar bet for me. The odds are one in two to the hundredth power, which is: one nonillion, 267 octillion, 650 septillion, 600 sextillion, 228 quintillion, 229 quadrillion, 401 trillion, 496 billion, 703 million, 205 thousand, three hundred and 76. Which, technically, is how many dollars you now owe me. You want to go double or nothing again? You still flip, I still call?"

"No thanks."

"Which means you accept it's happening, even though it's impossible."

"It means I've got no idea how you're manipulating a coin that came out of my pocket and that you've never touched and that I'm flipping, but it's the best magic trick I've ever seen."

"Problem being: it's not a trick."

"Mr. Field, there are plenty of things I don't know anything about. My daughter–she's in middle school–she already knows more than I ever did or will about history, science, art, and all that jazz. But I do work at a casino, so if there's one thing I understand, it's basic odds. Please don't insult my intelligence. If this is some kind of guerrilla audition for a show, it's working. I'm already a fan–you belong on the stage here. I'd be glad to introduce you to the program manager."

"We can do this all night, with any game of chance you want. Dice, cards, it doesn't matter. We can pick sports teams. Or how about this? Choose a number between one and 1,000,000, all right? A buck if I get it right."

"I don't want to play this game."

"But you picked one despite yourself, didn't you? A dollar says it's 3,261."

"Fuck me."

"Now," said Derek, leaning back on the high-top chair and tapping his empty glass to get Bert's attention, "you're starting to get it."

"You're fireproof?" said Shannon.

"No. At least, I don't think so. I think that if you could get me hot enough, I would burn. You just can't change my temperature enough to make me hot or cold."

"That's ..."

"Yeah, I know. Weird? Impossible?"

"I was going to say 'disappointing.' When you offered me your coat back at the club, I thought you were being chivalrous."

"I was!"

"That's not chivalry–chivalry means giving up something you actually need. If you didn't need the coat, then at best it was–thoughtful."

"Just so I'm clear," said Maxwell, "you're docking me points for offering you my coat while you were clearly freezing, because I happen to have a condition where I don't get cold."

"Hey, I didn't make up the definition of chivalry, so don't get mad at me when you don't live up to it. So, have you seen a doctor about this whole temperature thing?"

"Only the 100 or so that my mother marched me through, until one of them–this huge German with a handlebar mustache–told her that he had no idea what was wrong with me, and no one ever would, but that if she didn't want me spending the rest of my life as a freak in the medical circus, she should stop bringing me to doctors–because sooner or later one of them was going to use me to get famous. My mother–this was unusual for her–listened to him, kind of. She decided, by her own unique brand of logic, that if a normal doctor couldn't help me, that meant the condition was in my head. And if the condition was in my head, I needed a psychiatrist."

"Wait, so she thought you had a mental block against cold and heat?"

"You'd have to have met my mother to understand how something like that could seem totally rational to her. She basically picked the first psychiatrist she could find and sent me to him."

"Did he help you?"

"No, not at all–I mean, he didn't cure my condition. He had no more idea what was going on than anyone else. But it made my mother happy, I guess, to feel like she was doing something, so she kept sending me, and Dr. Gibbs is a stand-up guy, so I kept going. He doesn't even charge me any more. And it's been kind of–helpful, I guess–to have someone to talk things through with as my condition got worse. We mainly talk about its effects on the rest of my life. Like–with women, for example."

"It got worse? I totally take back what I said earlier about hoping for something more twisted, by the way–you have totally under promised and over delivered. This is way weirder than chicken blood infusions."

"Thanks, I think. But yeah, it got worse as I got older–you know what? I can show you. The waitress poured our coffees at the same time, right? From the same pot? Taste yours and tell me how hot it is."

"Like, lukewarm at best. Grounds for a lousy tip."

"Now sip mine."

Maxwell pushed his mug across the table, and Shannon stopped even before she took a sip, noting the steam that still skated and puffed on the surface.

"It's still hot because it was close to you?" she asked.

"It's still hot because it's *mine*. I could go to the bathroom for a half hour, and when I came back it would be exactly this temperature. I could put it outside. And it's not just hot things. I could put a cold beer in the microwave–a bottle of course, not a can, that would be dangerous–for twenty minutes. I've done it–there was still frost on the bottle."

Shannon laughed–and not the kind of laugh that Maxwell was used to hearing from a date. There was nothing nervous or derisive in her amusement–it was the laugh of a child delighted by the quarter a favorite uncle had just pulled from behind her ear.

"You like that?" said Maxwell, growing bold. "Then how about this: during the huge thunderstorm last August, when almost the whole city lost power, I discovered after three days that none of the food in my refrigerator had even started to turn. I haven't plugged the thing in since. I keep ice cream next to the bed and it's still frozen when I wake up and want a midnight snack. I can cook chicken by throwing it in a pan on the stove–no flame needed. I can boil water. I can leave a sheet of cookies in the oven while I sleep, and they're perfectly brown and gooey the next morning, or ..."

"You're like a superhero! Like the Human Torch or something."

"Yeah, right, only much, much lamer. I'm more like–the Human Thermostat, or the Human Pink Fiberglass Insulation Guy. Wait, how about the Human Thermos? Cold coffee and melted ice cream everywhere, beware!"

"Oh my God," said Shannon, covering her mouth with both hands for a second. "Oh. My. God. I've got it. Your superhero name should be one of those names that sounds like a normal name but has a double meaning, like Jack Hammer or Max Payne–and I know exactly what it should be. Are you ready for this?"

"I doubt it."

"Luke Warm."

"Amazing," Maxwell said.

"The Amazing Luke Warm? I think that's too much. Just Luke Warm is better."

"No, I mean *you're* amazing–I'm sorry, I don't want to freak you out, or say the wrong thing, it's just–you're taking this unbelievably well. This is never how it goes when I tell a girl about my condition. At first they just think I'm crazy, and if I actually *show* them they look at me like the world's biggest ... "

"I have hyperthymesia," said Shannon.

"Oh," said Maxwell, his mind taking a moment to brake fully, "right. And that's when ... which one is that again?"

"But for us–as psychiatrists, therapists, and other tenders to mental health–the most important consequence of the Hsiao Experiment is what it means for our patients. For example, I assume that most of you have read my first book, *The Suffering Decision*, and understood its central message–that there can be no suffering without the decision to suffer. But if every decision we make means we split the universe in two–one in which we chose one way, one in which we chose the other–think of the mental health consequences!

"Imagine being able to say to the relapsed alcoholic in front of you, bent almost double in his chair with shame, that in another universe he never took that drink the night before, and is, *at that very moment*, soberly and gratefully recalling his near miss?

"Imagine gently explaining to a woman, wracked with guilt, that in some other version of our world she never left her loving husband–whose only crime was a certain emotional distance characteristic of overachievement–to run off to New Hampshire with a soulless insurance salesman.

"For every version of us that decides to suffer, there is a version that refuses. For every version of us that ruins, injures, fails, there is one that repairs, heals, triumphs. Somewhere, we are each living the most perfect version of our lives.

"Explaining these concepts, relating the abstract details of quantum theory to the everyday pains and neuroses of everyday people–this must become the foremost function of the allied mental health professions–this function will dominate 'Psychiatry in a Post-Copenhagen World'–which, incidentally, is the sub-title of my book, available in the lobby or from any quality bookseller. There's a question in the back."

"Yes, Clarissa-in-your-head, Your Head."

"Clarissa? What are you doing here?"

"My question is this: isn't it true that you, and all your arguments, are full of shit?"

The crowd hissed and booed. Men and women turned in their seats, craning their necks to see who had spoken. A few even stood up. From the left someone shouted "Fie!"

"Wait," said Dr. Gibbs, holding out his hand to calm the crowd. "Quiet, please. Let us maintain academic decorum, even if she will not. Let her say what she has to say."

"After what I've just seen," Mr. Esposito said, "I'm not crazy about letting you back on the floor."

"I didn't come here to win," said Derek. "Those two bags I've got? I started the night with almost seven million dollars in there, and I plan to work my system until there's nothing left."

"That's very generous of you, Mr. Field, but–and don't take this the wrong way–I'd like to understand why you want to give Mohegan Sun all your money."

"Aren't all your guests here to give you their money? On average?"

"That's an interesting way to think about it, but usually they leave an element of chance in the equation."

Derek sighed.

"Look," said Mr. Esposito, "nothing would make me happier than to send you and your bags of cash back to the roulette wheel, but you freaked me out with all that coin flipping and number picking. I need to believe what you're telling me here. I *want* to. Make me a believer."

"You said you've got a daughter. Are you married?" Derek asked.

"For the moment, God help us both. You?"

"I was married to my job."

"Which is?"

"Was. Proprietary trader."

"You're one of those guys?" said Mr. Esposito. "I have some words for you about my pension fund–or what's left of it."

"I don't understand how a man who works at a casino can complain about Wall Street with a straight face. But proprietary traders have nothing to do with your pension fund. We invest on behalf of companies. We take their stacks of cash and turn them into bigger stacks."

"Sounds like the job you were born for."

"Can I get one more of these?" said Derek to Bert the bartender. Then, to Mr. Esposito: "You said you were married. If you won the lottery tomorrow, would you worry about whether your wife only loved you for your money?"

"Of course not."

"What if you found out tomorrow that you had won the lottery years ago, without realizing it, but she had known the whole time?"

"I don't get it–how could she have known I'd won the lottery if I didn't even know?"

"I don't know, she saw the ticket in your drawer or something. It doesn't matter–the point is, would you worry whether she had just married you for your money or not?"

Derek let Mr. Esposito chew on that for a few seconds, but then continued before he could answer.

"So now imagine you're a proprietary trader, and you're married to your job, and for years you think you're the best at it. The best in New York, which means you're the best in the world. And then one day

202

your mother asks you to buy her a lottery ticket while you're at the store–you would never buy one yourself, you think gambling is for degenerates–and you forget to give her the ticket. And it hits for seven million dollars."

"Wait, didn't you give your mom the ticket when it won?"

"Of course I gave her the ticket. But then I also bought another ticket, just as a joke. And I won again–the next week."

"And they didn't arrest you both on the spot?"

"They investigated my entire family, and now we're all barred from the lottery for life. But you're missing the point. I discovered that it wasn't just the lottery. Any game of chance–tossing coins, picking horses, blackjack, all these games I'd never played before–whatever it was, I won, always, 100 percent of the time, whenever money was on the line. So if my job–the job I was married to–the job I thought I was the best in the world at–is to pick stocks, how can I know whether I'm really any good? If I'm cursed to always win, how can I know I'm not actually a loser? Just like if you'd been rich when you met your wife–how could you have ever known that she didn't just love you for the money?"

"I could give away all the money and see if she stuck around."

"Just what I tried. I gave everything to charity, but I got it all back. I was still cursed. I've tried rituals from Africa, meditation, prayer. I read a book by this psychiatrist, claiming that suffering happens to us because we decide to let it, and that we can only *feel* cursed, not be cursed–and I started seeing him three times a week, hoping he could show me how to decide not to feel cursed."

"And?"

"Let's say it didn't work out that way. Now he has me flip unlucky coins and do these Native American cleansing chants. But I think finally–maybe–I've figured it out. With my roulette system the Curse is helpless–because I win every *spin*, but I lose *money* each time. It's turning the Curse against itself, you see? Just burning it out, spin by spin by spin. Evaporating it away."

Derek stopped and looked at Mr. Esposito. He clasped his hand in front of his chin, almost in the manner of a supplicant, until he noticed what he was doing and stopped.

"So what do you think?" Derek asked. "Are you a believer? Can I get back to that roulette table now?"

Mr. Esposito stood up, buttoning his suit jacket.

"Mr. Field, I still don't know how to explain what I've seen here tonight–and I don't really know whether I believe you or not," he said, "but I know one thing: you're sure as hell not going back to that roulette table."

"My turn to star in this freak show, I guess." said Shannon. "Name a date from our lifetimes, but not yesterday or anything–like, ten years ago or whenever."

"Okay, how about: June 3rd, 2002."

"Right. On June 3rd, 2002 I wake up and my clock says it's 6:28, two minutes before my alarm, and I'm pissed off about missing the extra sleep. The sun is coming in through a gap in the cardboard that my mother has folded and stuffed on the left side of the window to seal off the air conditioner–I figure the sun on my face is what woke me up and for a second I feel angry with her until I remind myself she was only trying to help. There's a glass of water half full on the nightstand next to my bed, which is white and has chips in the paint here, here, and here." Shannon closed her eyes and pointed to relative positions on the table, almost sticking her finger into her pancakes in the process.

"You have a photographic memory?" said Maxwell.

"I wish. The 3rd is my sister's birthday but we celebrated on the 2nd because both of us have to work, we got to the club at 11:22 and it was pretty empty. There's a girl wearing a leather skirt I really like at the bar, and she shoots me an evil look that makes me wonder whether I'm looking especially good or bad–I'm thinner back then. The guy next to her has an Abercrombie & Fitch shirt on, it's white with a blue collar. The next morning, the 3rd, my left toe is numb because of dancing in heels, and the numbness will last six days. It's two days before Elizabeth Smart gets kidnapped–I'll feel strange around the guy who does the lawn later that week–and five days before Serena beats Venus in straight sets at the French Open."

"Shannon."

"Yeah?"

"You remember all that?"

"I do."

"I mean ... how?"

"Pretty much anything that happens to me on a given date, I'll remember forever. The alarm goes off while I'm still fuming about waking up early ... sorry, once I get started it's hard to stop."

"You must have breezed through school."

"No, actually I have a shit memory."

"Yeah, no kidding–remember how you just told me you remember everything?"

"Everything that *happens* to me, not what I pay attention to. I remember what people wear, scores from baseball games I see, stuff like that. If I try to remember something on purpose, like what I read in a book, it's really hard–it's like there's no space or energy left. I spend way too much time thinking about the past, and I can't always control it–if someone names a date, or I see one written, it's there all of a sudden–all the details in my head. I take meditation classes to help me focus on the present and just, you know, *be* in the moment. It helps. I think it helps."

"And you've always had this? You were born with hyper ... "

"Hyperthymesia. Yeah. It's really rare–I'm one of like 21 cases ever documented. And I'm one of the lucky ones–mine is mild. Some people don't just *remember* everything, they *feel* it all again like it's happening for the first time. Can you imagine what that must be like? I mean, your cat dies and you can't ever get over it. But for the most part I can deal. I find ways to manage it, like I organize everything into buckets–Wednesdays, times I was wearing green, days when the Red Sox lost, and so on. It helps me deal with the flood of ... "

"Information."

"Yeah."

"Wow," said Maxwell, and immediately regretted it, though on reflection he could not think of anything better to have said. They both fell silent.

"So," said Shannon eventually.

"So?"

"This a deal-breaker? Too weird for you?"

"Are you kidding?" said Maxwell. "After what I just told you?"

"But your condition is harmless. And kind of cool. Mine is—it causes a lot of problems."

"Like?"

"Well, I'm not saying that you and I are going to turn into, you know, a *relationship* or anything—but people around me get tired of my remembering everything they do and say, and always being right about it, and it's worse with ..."

"Boyfriends?"

"Yeah."

"So what you're saying," said Maxwell, "is that if this works out I'll never be able to tell the same joke twice."

Shannon stared at him for a moment and smiled.

"Tell you what," she said, reaching across the table and taking his mug. "If this works out, you can recycle all the jokes you want, as long as I get your coffee whenever mine gets cold. Deal?"

"I'm going to need more than that if you get my coffee."

"Then counter-offer, jerk, I'm not going to negotiate with myself."

"I've got to carve out baseball stats. You can't correct my baseball stats in front of other people, even when you know they're wrong."

"I can live with that," Shannon said. "Deal?"

"Deal," said Maxwell.

They sat for a moment, suddenly awkward in each other's presence, unable to meet each other's eyes as Shannon sipped from Maxwell's coffee. When their eyes finally did meet, his cheeks turned red.

"You're blushing," said Shannon. "Can you feel it?"

"Not really," he said. "I mean, I can't feel anything in my cheeks, but I can kind of–tell that I'm blushing."

"Hey, I've got an idea," she said.

"What's that?"

"It's kind of a forward idea–for a first date, I mean."

"This doesn't exactly feel like a first date, does it?" said Maxwell. "To me it feels more like . . . "

"A third date?"

"Yeah."

"Then here's my idea: let's go back to your place and try a little competition. You try to make me forget what day it is, and I'll try to see if I can't change your temperature a little. Loser cooks breakfast."

"What's that thing," said Maxwell, clearing his throat, "that thing you're supposed to say when you want the check?"

"Check please?"

"That's it. You've got a good memory."

"So they tell me."

"Who's they?"

"Don't remember."

"Check please," said Maxwell.

"Let's start with the Hsiao Experiment itself," said Clarissa-in-his-head. "The problem isn't just that it's immoral and inhumane–or even that no impartial scientist ever had the chance to examine the box that Hsiao used before it was dismantled. The problem is that the Hsiao Experiment doesn't actually disprove the Copenhagen Interpretation."

"One in two to the 100th power isn't enough for you?" asked Dr. Sutherland in the front row. "Find me after the keynote–I have some wagers I'd like to propose." A ripple of laughter moved through the crowd until Dr. Gibbs shushed it.

"The odds don't matter," said Clarissa-in-his-head, "because we have no way to tell whether the Copenhagen Interpretation is wrong, but we were just lucky enough to be in the one parallel universe where that prisoner survived 100 pulls of the trigger–or whether the Copenhagen Interpretation is right, and there's just this one universe, in which this one prisoner was amazingly lucky."

"*Impossibly* lucky," said Dr. Sutherland.

"No more impossibly lucky than we would be to *happen* to inhabit the single universe, out of so many, in which he survived. The odds are one in two to the 100th in each case. We only know that one of them is the truth–it's a coin flip which one it is."

The crowd muttered as they considered this with their neighbors.

"I hate to admit it," Dr. Sutherland said finally, "but she has a point. Dr. Gibbs, will you rebut?"

Cries of encouragement erupted from the audience.

"Yes! Put her in her place!"

"Teach her a thing or two, Dr. G!"

"Does she even have an advanced degree, or did she stop after undergraduate?"

"Maybe if she spent a little less time crunching cold numbers like her insurance salesman husband, and a little more being nurturing and supportive, she'd still be married to you!"

Dr. Gibbs cleared his throat as if to speak, but without any idea what he would say.

"I'm not finished yet," said Clarissa-in-his-head. "Even if we stipulate that the Hsiao Experiment proves the existence of parallel universes, your so-called 'therapeutic ideas' are nonsense. You might just as well tell the relapsed alcoholic that in another universe he drank even more the night before and died in a gutter, while in another he drove home drunk and killed a teenager on the highway, while in yet another he had already relapsed the week before, and so on. For your one magical universe where everything has gone perfectly right for everyone, there are untold trillions of trillions where nearly everyone is mistaken, weak, and miserable nearly all the time. And this is what you hold up as your message of hope?"

"She's right," said a voice from the middle of the crowd, causing a minor gasp. "There would have to be all those universes where things went even worse."

"And doesn't it seem like there's always more ways for things to go wrong than right?" said someone from further up front. "So I guess there would be more unhappy universes than happy ones."

"But just the fact that there *is* a universe where everything has gone right," said Dr. Gibbs, "isn't that comforting?"

"You could even argue," Paul Sutherland said, "that if the Copenhagen Interpretation is wrong, then any decision at all just creates suffering. If you choose wrong, you suffer in this universe–and if you choose right, you suffer in another."

"That's very Buddhist," said someone from the back.

From the front: "It is, he's right–I took a survey class of world religions in college."

"Or maybe," continued Paul Sutherland, "the kindest and best thing you can do with your life is to decide to suffer yourself, so that some other version of you in some other universe doesn't have to."

"That's very Christian!"

"It is, he's absolutely right."

"Please," said Dr. Gibbs, "calm down, let us address these points rationally and one at a time, like scholars."

"This is bunkum!" cried a new voice, to much agreement, and the crowd exploded into a cacophony of reproach.

"Hokum!"

"Bullshit!"

"You're wasting our time!"

"Your first book was a fluke!"

"No, your first book was terrible!"

"You ruined your whole life over two patients. What about your other patients, the ones you stopped seeing? They needed your help too!"

"Did you ever even stop to think about your wife, and her feelings?"

"I'll bet you never put her first in anything, did you?"

"Did you even turn the gas off on the stove like she asked you?"

As Dr. Gibbs pleaded with them, the voices blended and diminished, like a background track of disapproval that someone was turning down slowly.

"I know what this means to you, Russell," said Clarissa-in-his-head, suddenly very quiet and very close, as if she had snuck up to the lectern and were speaking in his ear. "You think that if the Hsiao Experiment is real, you can explain Maxwell and Derek. But it's a dead end. There are too many holes, and even if you plug them all, it doesn't end up meaning anything. Wake up."

As she finished speaking, the cries from the crowd swelled again. Rotten produce rained down on the stage. A swollen melon exploded against the lectern, stinking of sulfur.

"Wait," Dr. Gibbs shouted over the voices, holding up his hands to protect himself from a cucumber, or as if appealing to a freight train, "just wait, let me respond from the beginning, let me think, please. Ah-ha, now I have it–now I have you!"

He came out from behind the lectern, weaving through the missiles, waving his arms, and stumbled down the aisle through the crowd, which quickly became dark and cavernous, searching for Clarissa.

"If the Copenhagen Interpretation is wrong, then there *has* to be one universe where the prisoner survives 100 pulls. But if the Copenhagen Interpretation is right, then it's almost impossible that *any* prisoner would ever survive. So, if the prisoner *did* survive, it's not a coin flip, because how can you not think it's more

likely that we're in a parallel–wait–this has to be right
…"

It was becoming quite dark, and his voice echoed around him.

"I appreciate the private room, Mr. Esposito," said Derek.

"My friends call me Espo. I can lift the house limit, as well."

"Thanks Espo, but I want to enjoy every minute of this."

"Another Sazerac, then? Something to eat? Our VIP chef is world-renowned for his porterhouse and baked Alaska."

"Maybe later. Right now I'd just like to get back to roulette."

Espo's cell phone rang from his breast pocket–the ring tone was the Imperial March from Star Wars.

"Pardon me a second," he said. "Hello? Delores, I can't talk now. No. I told you I would sign them, and I will. Soon. Soon means soon. I'm at work. Hold on–hold on–all right–just calm down, I'm going to call you right back, OK? Yes, right back. That means two minutes. Fine, two minutes *tops*. Bye."

Derek could hear an agitated voice still talking on the line as Espo hung up.

"I'm sorry about that," said Espo.

"Nothing to be sorry about."

"My soon-to-be-ex-wife–seems it can't be soon enough for her tastes. Let me tell you something, Derek: I'm glad I didn't know how bad divorce could be when I got married, because I'm not sure I would have gone through with it, and then I wouldn't have Jenny–my daughter. That's the great thing about kids–they put a cap on all your what-ifs and regrets, because you think 'If I'd done the right thing back then, or if this tough chance I was so mad about at the time had broken my way, then Jenny wouldn't exist today.' And that's just not on the table for me–I can't imagine life without Jenny, and I don't want to. Now her mother, that's a different story. But I guess you win some, you lose some. Or actually I guess *I* do–you, on the other hand."

The Imperial March started to play in his pocket again.

"I should probably go take this, or she'll just keep calling."

"You do what you have to do, Espo, and thanks again for everything. I'll see you later?"

The croupier set the ball spinning and followed it closely, watching for any indication that its orbit had begun to decay.

"Actually," said Espo, silencing his phone as the ball revolved, "do you mind if I stay and watch for a little while?"

"Knock yourself out," said Derek.

"No more bets," said the croupier.

In his dream Maxwell stood outside Demonologie, arms at his side, straight as a post around which a flood of naked women surged and swirled. There were women of every description and for every taste: tattooed biker chicks and scandalized debutantes covering themselves in the attitude of Botticelli's

214

Venus, librarians with their glasses on their heads shushing all who passed, madonnas weeping and rocking invisible babes at their breasts, blondes and brunettes and raven-hairs, every race and skin tone, fat and thin, girls from next door and across the tracks, flowing without impediment in and out of the club whose door Maxwell no longer manned.

Through the crowd he spotted something–or someone–a flash of red, familiar somehow. She entered the club and he followed, leaving his own clothes on the doorstep.

"It's all spelled out in my second book," shouted Dr. Gibbs into the dark, "in the case studies. Yes, yes, you aren't so bold now, are you? Derek thinks he's cursed because he wins every wager he makes, but it's just parallel universes at work. A man flips a coin and the universe splits in two. He wins in one universe and loses in the other. The winner flips again, and the universe splits again. Flip, split. Flip, split. No matter how long he keeps flipping, no matter how improbable his hot streak, in one universe the man will think he has won every toss he ever made. That just happens to be Derek, our Derek. Someone has to be that Derek–someone has to win every toss, every bet. It's inescapable.

"The same goes for Maxwell, but on an entirely different scale. He would scoff if I explained Derek to him, if I told him he had the same problem. 'Look,' he would say, 'Derek has some form of unruly luck I don't understand, whereas I have a physical condition. My problem is temperature, not luck.' But Maxwell is easily the luckiest man in our universe, so lucky that it doesn't even *look* like luck. Because temperature, considered correctly, is just a series of bets at a molecular level. He brings a hot cup of coffee into a cold room, and the odds are that the hot molecules of the coffee will transfer heat to the cold molecules of the room. The coffee will get colder and the room a little warmer. But there is some tiny, infinitesimal chance that the reverse will happen–that the room will transfer its scant energy into the coffee instead. The room will get colder and the coffee hotter. The odds against it are staggering, but they are just *odds*. It's a *bet*, so it works the same as Derek's so-called 'Curse.' Some version of Maxwell in some universe will win every one of these tiny bets of temperature."

A chilly breeze started blowing into Dr. Gibbs's eyes, as if a powerful air conditioning system had just flipped on.

"They both want me to cure them, but there's nothing to cure. In countless other universes they've already been 'cured.' When I gave Derek that 'unlucky coin' and had him flip it, in this universe it came up heads, and he was dejected. But in some other universe it came up tails, and he kissed the coin and embraced me in tears.

"If I were to tell Maxwell 'Hop on one foot until your condition goes away,' in most universes it would clear up immediately, leaving him amazed at the simplicity of my prescription. Or at some moment his 'condition' might simply vanish of its own accord, and he will attribute it to whatever he happened to be doing right then. Washing his hands? Oh, miraculous water from the men's room sink! Did he just sneeze? It must have all been a virus that he finally expelled the last traces of. But why are you wrinkling your noses? Why are you leaving?"

"Paul Sutherland, Yale University. Did you turn off the gas on the stove?"

"Yes, Paul, I ... either did or I didn't. It's 50/50. Rather, I did *and* I didn't. Maybe in this universe I did, not in another, or vice versa. It doesn't matter. It all averages out. But you are all missing the point! This is good news, my friends and colleagues, the best and gladdest news! We are unbelievably lucky to be here, not just in this universe but afloat in all of them, because somewhere, in some universe, everything is as it should be. Our sorrows are relieved and we, all of us, are perfectly happy together. In that best of all possible universes, even the dire pronouncements of the cosmologists are wrong–the universe is not winding down to entropy, and will never wind down. The sun will never quite burn out."

"But don't you think you should be more worried about this universe," asked Paul, "and whether or not you left the gas on here?" He sounded very far away.

"With all these other Copenhagens, it will happen eventually. It has to happen. You told me it had to happen, Clarissa. You had to leave. But another version of you ... you turned around when I called to you. Another version of me. You came back. You stayed. Do you think if we die, Clarissa, in this universe, we really go ... "

Derek wandered around the casino floor, unsure what to do with himself. He didn't feel any different–did that mean anything? He kept running through details, considering potential loopholes. What about the clothes on his back, for example, did they count against him? What about the tip he had given the croupier when his bankroll fell below the minimum bet? What about his cell phone, which he had left in the glove compartment of his rental? What about Dr. Gibbs's book, which he had left in the hotel room dresser instead of burning? Were these technicalities? Niggling points that would keep the Curse alive and well? He passed by the blackjack tables, sparsely populated but not empty even at this early hour, where he counted two 21s and four busts. Did that mean his aura was lucky or unlucky?

Eventually he found himself sitting by the slot machines. Their endless ringing and blinking lights soothed him, like the sound of a heavy rain on a cabin roof. They seemed to cancel out the precise frequency of his brain's worrying. He sat down on one of the stools.

Next to him a retiree was working his way through a long and delicate negotiation with one of the one-armed bandits, pausing every few pulls to gulp some oxygen from his tank-on-wheels. Beneath the straps of his rainbow suspenders he wore an ancient t-shirt on which cracked, screen-printed letters read "Have you thanked a veteran today?"

Derek could not stop watching as the old man pulled and pulled. It seemed that the old man was not even watching the reels tumble and slow to their conclusion, instead staring into space above the machine, relying on sound alone to know when it was time to pull again, or when a short spray of quarters needed to be cleared from the tray below. It seemed that he pulled the arm not to win but to pull the arm, and while the reels spun it was all he could do to wait to pull again, pull again, pull again.

Derek was not aware of how intently he had been staring until the old man became aware of it himself. Derek saluted him casually, but it was too late: the object of his fascination had been spooked, and after another pull or two, and a few glances over his shoulder, he wheeled his oxygen away to find another machine.

"Mr. Field," said Espo, having snuck up on Derek in the same fashion as at their first meeting, "you're more than welcome to stick around–I'm happy to comp you a few nights, if you'd like–but like I told you last night, I can't have you scaring off my guests."

"You know what's funny, Espo?" said Derek, not turning around. "He doesn't even want to win. Sure, if he won a million he'd freak out and jump up and down and maybe choke to death–but when the machine paid out a few bucks, he wasn't even happy. Like having to pick up the quarters was more of a nuisance than a victory."

"You're worried it didn't work," said Espo, walking around so they could speak face-to-face.

Derek didn't answer.

"There's only one way to find out. Here: allow me to stake you."

Derek looked at the quarter Mr. Esposito offered. Had he ever really looked at a quarter before? There were more ridges on the side than he would have guessed from memory, letters and numbers in odd places, a coppery slab sandwiched between two slices of silver.

"There's no point in putting it off," said Espo. "Come on, your friend already worked this one for you."

Derek stood and walked up to the machine the retiree had been playing. His mouth was dry and his hands trembling, but he dropped the quarter in the slot. The machine sprung to half-life, blinking and ringing quietly, waiting. He pulled.

"Don't turn away!" said Espo. "Watch!"

The reels clicked and tumbled, the lights flashed, a manic cowbell kept tempo deep in the guts of the machine. One by one the colored blurs began to cool and freeze.

Seven ...

Seven ...

Derek closed his eyes.

Maxwell woke up before Shannon, opening his eyes to her broad neck and shoulders and the brief tumble of red hair across them. He tried to slip quietly out from under the blankets he had put on the bed for her sake, but as his toes touched the pine floor he nearly screamed–he would have, in fact, if he had not inhaled involuntarily at the same moment. By the time he finally regained the breath to scream, reason had caught up with experience, and he understood that what he had just felt was not pain.

The feeling was not confined to his foot, either, though it was most intense there. This novel sensation assaulted his face and his chest and his arms, causing

hairs all over to stand up and urging him strongly to
urinate. Gasping and puffing, occasionally biting his
lip, he stepped gingerly across the floor and made his
way to the kitchen. There was something he had to
check.

He was still standing there, holding the door of
the fridge open, when he heard Shannon begin to stir
across the small apartment.

"Hey, I'm starving," she shouted. "Who does a girl
have to sleep with around here to get some breakfast?"

"With me," he called back, closing the refrigerator.
"But we'll have to go out. I don't trust these eggs."

Derek had never seen a morning so beautiful.
Even the puffy clouds of his breath seemed pure
and redeeming. He felt as if he had been drinking
champagne and dining on diamonds–or like a man
who had just received a revised diagnosis. He felt free.

"Sorry that took so long," said the valet as he
hopped out of Derek's rental, "Mr. Esposito asked me
to fill it up for you."

"Oh, thanks," Derek said. "I hadn't thought about
gas money. Shit, I don't have anything left for a tip
either."

"Already taken care of, Mr. Field."

"Hey," said Derek as he eased into the driver's seat.
"How many miles to New York City?"

"About 130 on a good day, sir."

"130 it is then."

For a moment Derek considered ducking back into
the casino and asking Mr. Esposito to comp him a suit,
so he could show up at his old boss's door in style.

But no, it was better this way: down to nothing, to the clothes on his back and a tank of gas in a rented car that he would have to return tomorrow, with only his talent to take on the world, to find out how good he really was.

As he pulled on to the highway, Derek put the radio on low and fished his cell phone out from the glove compartment. He had forgotten to switch it off, and the battery had been draining all night, but there was just enough charge left to chat for a few minutes. He dialed Dr. Gibbs, eager to tell him everything, now that it was too late for any concerns or objections. As the car heated up and the sun burst here and there over the bare tree line, Derek dialed again and again, hanging up and calling back each time the voice mail answered, just letting it ring and ring.

Acknowledgements

I am indebted to many friends who read and helped improve drafts of at least one of these stories: Eugene Barlow, Kevin Crowe, Drew Herbst, Ben Johnson, Meade Jorgensen, Dan Milstein, Matt Papi, and Owen Raccuglia. Thank you all.

Moira Racich designed the excellent cover.

Eric Yablonowitz read and commented helpfully on several drafts of several stories, even though he doesn't like short stories, earning my gratitude.

Alison Plante read the entire book and made numerous invaluable suggestions, for which I am extremely grateful.

Thank you to Jessica Werner, Robin Jorgensen, and Brian Jorgensen, who all read many stories in many incarnations and helped make them better.

A special shout out to Jessica Werner for profreading, in her copious free time, every single page but this one, and to Brian Jorgensen for his help formatting the print edition.

Most of all, thank you to my wife Mónica, for too much to list here.

About the Author

Edmund Jorgensen is the author of the novel *Speculation* and the short story collection *Other Copenhagens (And Other Stories)*.

He lives in Watertown with his wife and empirically adorable son.

If that's not enough for you, you can find out more about him (and sign up for his email list) at http://www.inkwellandoften.com.

He goes by @tomheon on Twitter, and welcomes email at ewj@inkwellandoften.com.